中英雙語典藏版

象徵主義文學代表作
影響法國的五十本書之一

青鳥

L'Oiseau Bleu

比利時的莎士比亞

莫里斯·梅特林克

（Maurice Maeterlinck）——著

喬治特·萊勃倫克——改編

肖俊風——譯　詹艷玲——繪

晨星出版

目錄

CONTENTS

第1章
樵夫小屋

　　今天是平安夜，媽媽把吉爾和梅蒂在床上安頓好，然後吻了吻兄妹倆。今天的吻比平常顯得更加深情。由於風雪太大，爸爸好幾天沒到林子裡去砍柴了，因此媽媽沒錢買聖誕禮物，兄妹倆床頭的長襪子裡依然空空的，媽媽想到這兒就很難過。很快兩個孩子就進入了夢鄉，四周靜悄悄的，只能聽到時鐘的嘀嗒聲、貓的呼嚕聲、狗的鼾聲。突然，一道亮如白天的光從百葉窗的縫隙中溜了進來，桌子上的燈自動亮了。孩子們醒了，揉揉眼睛，伸了個懶腰，打了個哈欠，哥哥悄悄地問妹妹：

　　「梅蒂？」

　　「嗯，哥哥。」梅蒂也醒了。

　　「妳睡著了嗎？」

　　「你呢？」

　　吉爾說：「還沒，睡著了怎能跟妳說話呢？」

　　「聖誕節到了嗎？」梅蒂問。

　　「還沒，明天才是聖誕節。可是聖誕老人今年不會帶禮物給我們了。」

　　「為什麼呢，哥哥？」

　　「媽媽沒有上街去請他來，但是媽媽說聖誕老人明年一定會來。」

「明年聖誕節還要等好久吧？」

「要好長好長的時間呢，可是今天晚上聖誕老人會去看對面有錢人家大房子裡的孩子們！」吉爾歎了一口氣說。

「真的嗎？」

「噢，媽媽忘了關燈！」吉爾突然叫著說「我們起床！」

「不行，這樣不行呀！」梅蒂忘不了媽媽的話，她一直是個聽話的孩子。

「這兒又沒有別人，為什麼不行呢？看見百葉窗了嗎？」

「噢，好亮啊！」

「一定是晚會的燈光！」

「什麼晚會？」

「對面有錢人家的孩子們正在舉行晚會，那是他們家聖誕樹上的燈光。打開百葉窗吧。」

「可以嗎？」梅蒂怯怯地問。

「又沒有人阻攔我們，當然可以啦！快起來吧，妳聽到音樂聲了嗎？」

兄妹倆跳下床，跑到窗前，爬上凳子，掀起百葉窗簾。整個小屋亮了起來，他們倆急切地望向窗外。

「嘿！」吉爾說：「我們什麼都看得到！」

「我什麼也看不到呀！」小梅蒂說。凳子上幾乎沒有多大地方可以讓她站。

「有兩輛馬車，每輛車有六匹馬。外面正在下雪呢！」

「有十二個小男孩從車上下來！」小梅蒂努力地往窗外望。

「不對！是十二個小女孩。」

「可是他們穿的都是男孩子的褲子！」

「噓！別大聲嚷嚷……你看！是聖誕樹！」

「那些掛在樹枝上的金色東西是什麼呢？」

「當然是玩具！」吉爾說：「有寶劍、槍、大炮、士兵……」

「那滿滿一桌子是什麼？」梅蒂又問。

「水果、糕點，還有奶油餡餅。」

「嘿！」梅蒂禁不住拍著小手「他們穿得多好看啊！」

「他們還笑得很開心呢！」吉爾也看得入迷了。

「他們在跳舞呢！」

「對啊！」吉爾喊道：「我們也跳吧！」

於是兄妹倆高高興興地在凳子上蹺起腳來。

「哈！真好玩啊！」梅蒂說。

「那些孩子們就要吃糕點了，他們已經拿到手裡了！」吉爾叫著說，「多香呀，他們在吃啦，他們在吃啦！……噢，好棒啊！」

梅蒂想像著，彷彿自己的手中也有了糕點。「我有十二塊！」

「我的更多，有四個十二塊！」吉爾叫著，「不過我會分給妳的。」

兄妹倆就這樣沈浸在別的孩子的幸福之中，忘記了自己的貧困。他們高興得跳著、笑著、叫著。突然，一陣響亮的敲門聲，

兄妹倆都吃了一驚，不再跳了，一動也不敢動。那厚重的木門閂嘎吱吱地自動抽了起來，門慢慢開了。一個身材矮小的老太太走了進來，她戴著一頂紅帽子，穿一身綠衣服，只有一隻眼睛，鷹勾鼻子都快要碰到下巴了。她手裡拄著一根拐杖，駝著背，瘸著腿——她是一位仙女吧！

老太太一瘸一拐地走到兄妹倆面前，用濃濃的鼻音問道：「你們這兒有青鳥嗎？」

「哥哥有一隻鳥。」梅蒂說。

「但這是我的鳥，不能送人。」吉爾趕緊接著說。

仙女戴上一副又圓又大的眼鏡，看了看吉爾的那隻鳥。

她大聲說道：「我要的是一隻真正的青鳥，這隻鳥的顏色不夠青。我的小女兒需要青鳥，她病得很重……」仙女將她彎彎的手指湊近長長的鼻子，壓低聲音，用一種神祕的口氣悄聲說：「你們知道嗎？青鳥就意味著幸福。我的小女兒如果得到了青鳥，病就會好了，也就是得到了幸福。因此我命令你們去替她找青鳥，你們必須馬上就出發……你們知道我是誰嗎？」

吉爾和梅蒂迷惑不解地互看一眼，然後吉爾很有禮貌地說：「您和我們的鄰居柏林考脫太太很像。」

柏林考脫太太有一個小女兒，十分可愛，禮拜天總是和小兄妹一起玩。不幸的是，這位長著一頭美麗金髮的小女孩，得了一種怪病，讓她常常躺在床上。當她躺在病床上的時候，總想要跟吉爾的鴿子玩，可是吉爾很喜歡這隻鴿子，捨不得把鴿子送給小女孩。現在聽說仙女的女兒病了，想要青鳥，吉爾覺得這些狀況

跟柏林考脫太太家的情形很像，所以就把仙女當成柏林考脫太太。

讓吉爾驚訝的是，仙女聽了他的話竟氣得滿臉通紅。仙女問吉爾：「我長得怎麼樣？是美還是醜？是老還是年輕？」

她這樣問的用意無非是考驗吉爾，看他是否真誠善良。吉爾不敢看她，也不敢說出心裡的話。於是老太婆高聲說道：「我是仙女蓓麗呂！」

仙女見兩個孩子穿著睡衣，便要他們換上外出的衣服。她一邊幫梅蒂穿上衣，一邊問道：「妳爸爸媽媽在哪兒？」

「他們都在那兒睡覺。」梅蒂指著右邊的房門。

「那妳的爺爺和奶奶呢？」

「都去世了。」

「那麼……你們有兄弟姊妹嗎？」

「有三個弟弟！」吉爾回答說。

「還有四個妹妹。」梅蒂隨後補充說。

「他們都在哪兒？」

「都死了。」吉爾說。

「那麼你們想見見他們嗎？」

「想！現在就讓我們見見他們吧！」

仙女說：「我又沒有把他們裝在口袋裡！但是你們很幸運，當你們經過懷念國的時候，就能夠看見他們了。懷念國就在你們去找青鳥的路上，往第三個路口左轉……剛才我敲門時，你們在做什麼呢？」

「我們正在玩『吃蛋糕』的遊戲。」吉爾說。

「你們有蛋糕嗎？在哪兒？」

「在有錢人孩子的家裡。您過來看看，那蛋糕真棒！」

吉爾拉著仙女走到窗前。

「那是別人在吃蛋糕呀！」仙女說。

「沒錯」吉爾說：「不過我們可以看著他們吃呀！」

「你們不生他們的氣嗎？」

「為什麼要生他們的氣？」

「因為他們沒有把蛋糕分給你們，蛋糕全被他們吃了！這一點兒也不公平。」

「沒什麼，他們有錢嘛！妳看，他們的屋子多漂亮。」

「你們這兒也一樣漂亮，只是你們看不見罷了。」

「不！看得見！我的視力非常好」吉爾說：「教堂鐘樓上的房間我都能看得清清楚楚，爸爸就看不大清楚！」

仙女突然有些生氣，她大聲地說：「我說你們確實看不見！」

她的火氣越來越大。吉爾想：對仙女來說，似乎能看清楚教堂鐘樓上的時間是一件十分要緊的事。

仙女當然知道吉爾的眼睛能看到東西，但她想教吉爾認識身邊萬物內在的善與美。因為他是個善良的孩子，應該獲得幸福。但這可不是件容易的事。她知道，很多人枉活一世，始終沒有享受過就在他們身邊的幸福。她是一個法力無窮的仙女，於是決定給吉爾一頂鑲嵌著魔法鑽石的帽子。這顆鑽石有一種奇異的功

能：展現事物的真理。有了這顆鑽石，吉爾就能看清楚事物內在的本質，就會認識到每一種事物都有生命，有靈魂，就像人類一樣，是為了配合人類的生活，使人們生活得更幸福。

仙女從她揹著的大袋子裡取出一頂綠色的小帽子。帽子上面有一個白色帽徽，帽徽的中央嵌著一顆雪亮的大鑽石，吉爾高興極了。仙女告訴他怎樣使用鑽石：只要一按鑽石，就能看見事物的靈魂；將鑽石轉向右邊，就能看見過去；轉向左邊，就能夠看到未來。

吉爾一臉興奮，樂得合不上嘴，又蹦又跳。過了一會兒，他又擔心這頂帽會子落在別人手中，他叫道：「爸爸會把它拿走的！」

「不會的。只要你把它戴在頭上，就沒有人能看見它。」仙女說，「戴上試試看！」

「咦」吉爾和梅蒂拍著手歡呼：「真的看不見了！」

吉爾剛戴上帽子，眼前的一切馬上都變了樣，老仙女變成了年輕又美麗的公主，戴著閃閃發光的珠寶，穿著綢緞衣服；小屋的牆壁變得像寶石似地晶瑩發亮；破舊的家具變得像大理石一樣閃著光澤。吉爾和梅蒂高興得歡呼起來，邊拍手邊跳。

但是，讓他們更驚訝的事還在後頭。你瞧！爺爺留下的那口大鐘此時打破了沈寂，小屋一時間響起了最最美妙的音樂聲。大鐘裡走出來十二個服飾豔麗的舞者，圍在吉爾和梅蒂周圍笑著、唱著，跳起舞來。

仙女說：「這就是你們生活中的十二個小時！」吉爾讚佩地

看著這些美麗的小精靈像小鳥般輕盈地飄來飄去。

突然間一個的滑稽的胖傢伙，掙扎著從麵包鍋裡爬出來。他身上沾滿麵粉，上氣不接下氣，躬著身向兄妹倆行禮。是麵包先生！其他的麵包也跟著爬了出來，他們快樂地和十二個小姑娘們跳起舞來，白色的麵粉四處飛揚，彷彿在白霧之中漫舞，絲毫沒注意滿身的麵粉灑到那些姑娘身上。

麵包先生們和十二小時姑娘跳起了華爾茲；盤子們、玻璃杯們、叉子和刀子也來湊熱鬧，乒乒乓乓地互相碰撞，吵得不得了。

大家鬧得正起勁的，一條巨大的火舌從煙囪裡忽地竄出來，將整個屋子照得閃閃發亮，房子好像著火了。大家驚慌失措，全都躲到角落去了。兄妹倆都嚇哭了，急忙藏到仙女的衣襟下。

「這是火先生，別怕！」仙女說：「他人很好，也是來湊熱鬧的，不過他脾氣太暴躁，你們可千萬別碰他！」

眼前立著一個紅臉大漢，當他揮舞長長的手臂時，肩上的那些絲巾就飄然而動，好像一道道火苗在搖曳。他的頭髮一縷縷地直立著，閃閃生輝。他開始狂熱地舞動四肢，在屋裡跳來跳去。

仙女蓓麗呂拿出魔杖輕點了一下水龍頭，一位年輕美麗的姑娘如同清泉一般飄然而至。她就是溫柔美麗的水姑娘，她只穿著睡衣，但奔湧而出的清水像一件晶瑩剔透的外衣。她看見火先生還在那裡興高采烈地旋轉，便怒氣沖沖地奔向火先生，用盡全力向他噴呀，潑呀，一直澆得他濕淋淋的。火先生也大發雷霆，不斷地冒著煙。

突然「砰」的一聲，把吉爾和梅蒂嚇了一跳，瓷器破碎的聲音傳了過來，他們同時朝桌子望去。真教人意外！牛奶罐掉在地上碎成了一堆，一位美麗的小姐從碎片之中顯現出來。牛奶小姐雙手緊緊握在一起，有點膽怯地叫了一聲，然後抬起頭來，用懇求的目光看著大家。

這時，用藍色糖紙包著的糖塊，似乎也有了生命。只見他用力地左右掙扎，一隻細長的胳膊從糖紙裡伸了出來，隨後是一個尖腦袋撐破糖紙鑽了出來，接著又出來一隻胳膊和兩條不知有多長的腿。哈哈哈！糖先生那滑稽的模樣逗得吉爾和梅蒂大笑起來。

「汪汪！汪汪……你們好！你們好！我們總算可以交談了，我的兩位小主人！不管我平時怎樣搖尾巴，怎樣叫喊，你們就是不懂我的意思，噢，我愛你們，我多愛你們呀！」

兄妹倆馬上就認出了他：他是狗先生蒂魯。每當吉爾和梅蒂進入樹林，他總是伴隨在他們左右。他忠誠地守衛著家門，是最值得信賴、最真摯的朋友。現在他直立著走來，後腿顯得有點兒短，兩隻前爪舉在胸前不停地擺動，像笨手笨腳的小孩子在蹣跚學步。他吻了吉爾後又去吻了梅蒂,把他的兩位小主人稱作他的小上帝,此情此景實在是讓人動情!

貓女士蒂勒脫也變成了人,兄妹倆親切地拍撫著蒂勒脫時,狗先生心裡非常地難受。

貓女士又舔又蹭,擦亮雙爪,然後泰然自若向梅蒂伸出一隻手,「小姐!早安,今天您看起來氣色真好!」梅蒂和吉爾拍撫著她。

這時發生了一件極不尋常的事情,時間正是午夜十一點,是冬夜中最黑暗的時刻。突然有一道亮光射進屋裡,如同正午的太陽一樣照得屋裡一片通明。

亮光形成的一個巨大光環從窗戶射進來,一位光彩奪目、無比可愛的少女在光環的正中央緩緩地顯現。少女身上披著華麗的輕紗,卻絲毫無法掩飾少女的美貌。她的雙臂光潔晶瑩,似乎是透明的,若有若無;她那雙明亮的大眼睛對所有的人都柔情脈脈。

「是女王!」吉爾叫起來。

「不是的,是光仙子!孩子們。」仙女說。

　　光仙子微笑著朝兩個孩子走來。她是賦予大地力量與美的源泉，是天國的光芒。雖然她是前來執行一項渺小的任務，但她卻十分自豪，那就是教導孩子們認識另一種光──心靈之光。

　　「啊，光仙子！」不論是靜物還是動物都齊聲歡呼。他們都喜歡她，所以圍著光仙子又笑又跳。吉爾和梅蒂高興得手舞足蹈。他們從來沒想過能夠參加今天這樣美妙有趣的晚會，因此叫嚷得比誰都大聲。

　　突然，隔壁傳來了三下敲牆的聲音，聲音大得幾乎快把房子震倒！是爸爸在敲牆。爸爸被歡鬧聲吵醒了，要來制止他們。這是遲早會發生的事，現在果然發生了。

　　「快轉鑽石！」仙女對吉爾喊道。

　　吉爾立刻執行命令，可是他還不能熟練轉動鑽石。他一想到爸爸要過來手就顫抖，一點也不聽使喚，幾乎要把鑽石下面的帽徽給弄壞了。

　　「慢點兒！慢點兒！」仙女喊著說，「天哪，你轉得太快了！假如大家來不及恢復原來的樣子，我們的麻煩就大了！」

　　屋裡一瞬間亂糟糟的。牆壁一下子失去了光彩；大家連忙到處亂竄，急著恢復原形。火先生找不到煙囪；水姑娘跑著尋找她的水龍頭；糖先生站在撕碎了的包裝紙面前痛苦不已；最大個頭的那個麵包用盡力氣也擠不回鍋裡去，其他比他個兒小的麵包早已亂七八糟地擠進鍋裡，把地方都占了；狗先生剛才的身體太長，原來的狗窩早已容不下他了；貓女士也不例外，怎麼也鑽不進原來下榻的籃子了；只有十二小時姑娘們毫不耽擱地溜回到鐘裡，因為她們平時就習慣跑在別人的前面。

　　光仙子泰然自若地站在那裡一動也不動，想為大家樹立一個沈著冷靜的榜樣。但她那鎮靜自若的態度沒起一點兒作用，還沒復原的幾位圍著仙女又哭又叫：「有什麼危險嗎？我們該怎麼辦？」

　　「好吧，我就告訴你們實話。」仙女說：「凡是陪同吉爾和梅蒂去找青鳥的，任務完成後就會死去。」大家聽了全都傷心地哭了起來。只有狗先生蒂魯沒哭，他樂於繼續保持人的形狀，多久都沒有怨言，而且他也學著光仙子的樣子，表示自己一定要幫兩位小主人開路。

　　「聽！爸爸又在敲牆！他起來了！」吉爾叫道：「我都能聽到他的腳步聲了！」

　　「明白了嗎？」仙女說：「你們已沒有選擇的餘地，不能再拖延了，必須馬上跟我們一同出發。你們先到我家，我要幫你們打扮打扮，穿上得體的衣服，從這兒出去吧！」

　　說完，仙女用手中的魔杖指向窗戶。那窗戶頓時神奇地往下伸展，變成了一扇門。等他們一個個躡手躡腳地走出去後，窗戶馬上又恢復了原狀。就這樣，在這個美妙的平安夜，在紀念耶穌誕生的鐘聲裡，在明亮皎潔的月光下，吉爾和梅蒂啟程去尋找能給他們帶來幸福的青鳥了。

第 2 章

仙女宮殿

　　一行人還沒走上大路，仙女便意識到他們無法這個樣子穿過村子。過節時的夜晚，村子裡燈火通明，人們很容易發現他們。仙女在吉爾的頭上輕輕地拍了拍，想讓他們借助法力到達她的宮殿。頓時一群螢火蟲如雲團一樣把這一行人團團圍住，然後輕輕托向天空。當他們還在為仙女的魔法驚訝的時候，他們已經抵達仙女的宮殿了。

　　「跟我走。」仙女說，並領著他們走過一個個用金銀裝飾的廳堂和走廊，來到了一個大房間，四壁都是鏡子，房間裡有個很大的衣櫃，屋內光線沿著衣櫃的凹痕攀爬而上。仙女蓓麗呂從口袋裡掏出一把鑽石鑰匙，將衣櫃打開，所有的人都驚訝地叫起來！各國的奇裝異服、鑲著寶石的斗篷、翡翠項鏈、珍珠頭飾、紅寶石手鐲……吉爾和梅蒂從未見到過這麼多貴重的東西，狗呀貓呀，以及那些靜物們看了這些珍寶更是目瞪口呆。

　　火先生很快相中了一身飾有金片的紅衣服，因為他對紅色情有獨鍾，而且他不想戴任

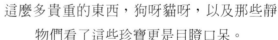

何頭飾，因為他的腦袋總是熱騰騰的。糖先生生選了一件藍底白花的衣服，一頂圓錐形的尖帽子，穿戴起來顯得十分好笑。貓女士選了一套繡花的黑色緊身衣，披了一件長長的天鵝絨斗篷，又把一頂騎士帽戴在小腦袋上，帽上插著一支長羽毛；她腳上穿了一雙軟質小山羊皮靴——為了紀念她那大名鼎鼎的前輩「穿靴子的貓」；而前爪則戴上一副手套，防止在路上沾上灰塵。

然後，貓女士邀請糖先生和火先生去呼吸點新鮮空氣。

趁著大夥兒還忙著穿戴打扮的時候，這三個密友離開了房間，穿過幾道漂亮的走廊，來到一個大廳裡。貓女士壓低嗓門：「我帶你們到這裡來，是想要討論一下我們三個目前的處境。我們沒多少自由時間了，我們要盡可能地利用最後這點兒時間……」

一陣狗叫聲打斷了她的演說。

「汪汪汪！」

「聽！」貓女士喊道。「是那條傻狗！他嗅到了我們的氣味，就連片刻安寧也不行。我們躲到欄杆後面吧！最好別讓他聽到我對你們說的話。」

「太遲了！」糖先生站在門口說。

可不是？蒂魯高興地衝了進來，喘著粗氣，又跳又叫。

貓女士一看到狗先生，忍不住一陣厭惡，轉身就走。「瞧他那套衣服！活像『灰姑娘』故事中車夫穿的制服！他也只配穿這樣的衣著，一副天生的奴才相！」

說完，她捋了捋觸鬚，輕蔑地「嘶嘶」了幾下，站到火先生和糖果先生之間，流露出一種鄙夷的神情。狗先生蹦蹦跳跳地轉來轉去，那副模樣實在是讓人忍不住笑了出來！每逢他轉身時，天鵝絨的上衣便像旋轉木馬一般飛轉起來，衣襟下擺飄然而開，露出一條粗壯的尾巴來。

「瞧，瞧呀！多漂亮！」蒂魯叫道：「看看這花邊和刺繡！這可都是真的金子啊！」他一點也沒有察覺別人在嘲笑他；他腳上穿著黑漆皮馬靴，由於兩隻前爪經常使用，因此蒂魯不聽別人的勸告，始終不肯戴手套。蒂魯生性落拓不羈，一時改不了習性，此刻他正趴在大廳的臺階上，嗅嗅牆腳，撓撓地面。

突然間一陣悅耳的女高音從遠處傳來，這充滿活力的歌聲越來越近，在高高的拱門外回盪。接著，水姑娘出現了，銀光閃閃的衣裙飄逸動人，飾有珊瑚的一頭秀髮垂至小腿。

一見到水姑娘，火先生現出粗俗兇惡的嘴臉，他嘲笑著說道：「哼！她就差沒拿一把雨傘了！」

水姑娘說起話來更是風趣。她知道火鬥不過水，瞅了瞅火先生又紅又亮的大鼻子，不氣不惱地打趣他說：

「你剛才說什麼？是不是在說幾天前我看見的那個大紅鼻子？」

在場的所有人都笑了起來，火先生的臉又紅又燙像顆火炭。

一個滑稽可笑、臃腫不堪、打扮得五顏六色的大塊頭走過來，把往大廳的通道堵住了，那就是大腹便便的麵包先生。麵包先生興高采烈地說：「我來了！我來了！你們覺得我穿的這身藍鬍子式的衣服怎麼樣？」

狗先生歡快地圍著麵包先生跳來跳去。他覺得麵包的樣子太棒了！那件佈滿銀色月牙的黃天鵝絨長袍，使蒂魯想起他最愛吃的馬蹄麵包捲。麵包先生的頭巾又大又豔麗，多像一個精製的圓麵包！

「太美了！太美了！」狗先生不停地讚歎。

牛奶小姐羞答答地跟在麵包先生的後面。儘管仙女為她挑了許多漂亮衣服，她還是愛穿奶油色的服裝。

貓女士專橫地打斷了大家：「少廢話了，聽我說，時間緊迫，我們的未來不妙啊！」

大家看著貓女士，有些迷惑不解。貓女士有些不耐煩，她接著說：「仙女已說過了，等這次旅行一結束，我們也就沒命了。因此，我們必須不擇手段，盡量拖延時間。」

麵包先生急忙表示贊同貓的意見，狗先生站心裡憤憤不平，裝作什麼也沒聽見。貓女士這時接著說：「我們應該想盡一切辦法，阻止孩子們找到青鳥，即便這麼做會危及吉爾和梅蒂的生命！」狗先生一向憑良心辦事，聽了貓女士的這些話，撲過來就想咬她。火先生、糖先生和麵包先生立即過來勸解。

　　「別亂！別亂！我是會議主席！」麵包先生十分自負地出來維持秩序。

　　火先生怒氣沖沖地發問：「誰選你當主席啦？」

　　「誰讓你出來干涉的？」水姑娘質問道，她將濕漉漉的頭髮甩在火先生身上。

　　「抱歉！」糖先生用調解的口氣哆嗦著說，「抱歉！現在是重要時刻，我們應當心平氣和地討論。」

　　「我非常同意糖果先生和貓女士的意見。」麵包先生說。

　　「你們都太不像話了！」狗先生齜著牙大聲說，「這事應該讓人類來決定，我們必須聽從人類，此外別無選擇！我只認同人類，人類叫我做什麼我就做什麼。人類永存！人類萬歲！為人類活著，為人類獻身！人類就是一切！」

　　貓女士嗓子尖，她的聲音蓋過了在場所有的人。「在場的各位！」貓女士大聲說道：「不管是動物還是靜物都有靈魂，人類卻從不知道這一點。正是由於他們不知道我們有靈魂，我們才能保留這麼一丁點的自由。要是他們找到了青鳥，那麼他們就會知道一切、看到一切，我們就只好完完全全任他們擺佈了。別忘了過去我們四處遊蕩，何等自在，想到哪兒去就到哪兒去！」突

然，貓女士突臉色大變，壓低嗓門：「噓！當心！我聽到仙女和光仙子的腳步聲了。大家都知道，光仙子總是支持人類，站在人類那一邊，因此她是我們危險的敵人，大家留神點！」

仙女一邁進門檻就感到不大對勁。她大聲問：「你們躲在角落裡幹什麼呢？你們簡直就像一群圖謀不軌之徒！」

兄妹倆手拉著手站在仙女面前，華麗的服裝讓他們覺得有些不自在。他們稚氣地互相投以羨慕的目光。

梅蒂穿了一件繡著粉紅花朵、佈滿金色亮片的黃色絲綢連衣裙。她頭上戴著一頂橘紅色天鵝絨帽子，肩上披著很薄的披巾。吉爾穿著用天鵝絨做成的紅色上衣、藍色燈籠褲，頭上仍舊戴著那頂神奇的帽子。

「青鳥有可能就藏在你們的爺爺奶奶家。」仙女對大家說：「因此你們應該先去懷念國。」

「可是他們已經死了。」吉爾問：「我們怎樣才能見到他們呢？」

仙女解釋說他們不會真的死去的，只要他們的孫子、孫女仍在懷念他們。

「人類不知道這個秘密。」仙女又說：「不過吉爾現在有了帽子上那顆鑽石，所以你會明白：有的人雖然去世了，但是只要有人還在懷念他們，他們就會像從前一樣幸福地活著。」

「你也和我們一起去嗎？」吉爾轉過身來問光仙子。光仙子正站在門口，整個大廳都被照得通明。

「她不去，光仙子是無法回顧過去的。」仙女回答說，「她得把力量貢獻給未來。」

　　吉爾和梅蒂就要出發了，還沒有上路他們就覺得十分饑餓。仙女立刻吩咐麵包先生給他們準備些吃的。這個胖乎乎的傢伙看到自己能擔負如此重大的責任，十分得意。於是他抽出彎刀、解開長袍上的扣子，從肚子上切了兩片遞過來，孩子們高聲地笑了起來。糖先生雖然非常小氣，但是爲了給大家留個好印象，扳下兩根手指遞給了兄妹倆。兩個孩子都十分驚訝。

　　當大家都走向門口的時候，仙女把他們叫住了。

　　「吉爾和梅蒂必須單獨去，其餘的人今天不要去，有你們陪伴並不合適。他們要和爺爺、奶奶一起度過一個夜晚，因此你們幾個先到一邊去。再見了，親愛的吉爾和梅蒂，再見了孩子們。記住一定要按時歸來，這一點非常重要。」

　　孩子們提著大鳥籠，手拉著手走出了大廳。他們的動物、靜物朋友們在仙女指揮下排列成行，返回宮殿。只有狗先生蒂魯沒有聽命令，他聽到仙女說要兩個孩子自己去，就暗下決心無論如何也要跟著去照顧他們。因此在其他人忙著告別時，他悄悄躲在門後。但是這個可憐的傢伙沒想到仙女的法眼是無所不見的。

　　「蒂魯！蒂魯！你給我過來！」可憐的狗先生一向服從命令，不敢違抗，只好夾著尾巴加入了回宮殿的隊伍。看著兩位小主人在金光閃閃的大樓梯上消失時，狗先生禁不住絕望地哀號起來。

第 3 章
懷念國

懷念國並不遙遠，但是他們必須穿過一片森林才能到達懷念國。那森林終年籠罩在濃霧之中，森林裡的大樹古老而且茂密，高的望不到樹稍。如果仙女沒先跟孩子們說：「只有一條路，要一直向前走。」他們倆肯定會在森林裡迷路。

地面上開滿了同一種花兒，像鋪上了花地毯，全是雪白的紫羅蘭。由於見不到陽光，花兒雖然很漂亮，可是沒有香味。

孩子們邊走邊採集美麗的鮮花。他們不知道，紫羅蘭是一種思念的花，每採一枝，他們離爺爺奶奶就近一步。沒多久，他們來到了一棵掛著告示牌的高大橡樹下。吉爾擱下手中的鳥籠，沿著裸露的樹根爬上去，告示牌上寫著：

> **懷念國**

吉爾欣喜若狂地叫了起來：「到了，我們到了！」

他們確實到了懷念國，可是他們四下張望，什麼也看不見。梅蒂嗚嗚地哭了起來：「我什麼也看不見！我又冷又累！再也不想走了！」這時吉爾驚喜地大叫：「咦！你看那邊！你快看！霧散了！」

眼前的霧果然開始散去，就像薄紗般被一隻無形的大手揭去。遮天蔽日的大樹慢慢地消失，眼前出現一間爬滿常青藤的美麗農家小屋。小屋座落在開滿鮮花的院中，四周的樹上結滿了果子。

孩子們一下子就認出了門口的那條看門狗、果園裡那頭可愛的棕色乳牛，還有柳條籠子裡的畫眉鳥。一切都沐浴在淡淡的陽光之中，氣氛溫馨極了。

這裡就是懷念國！兄妹倆驚異地在那裡站著，他們打定主意：既然找到路了，以後要經常來這裡看看。霧已經散盡了，他們看見爺爺奶奶就坐在不遠處的凳子上打著瞌睡。

「找到了！找到他們了！那不就是爺爺奶奶！」

他們聽到奶奶微微發顫的話語聲：「我有一種感覺，那兩個活在人間的孫兒、孫女今天來看我們了。」

爺爺對她的話表示贊同：「我能感覺得到，他們一定懷念著我們，現在我有些坐立不安。」

話還沒說完，吉爾和梅蒂就投入了爺爺奶奶的懷抱。多麼驚喜啊！他們盡情地親吻著，擁抱著，這種幸福感是無法用語言來表達的。他們高興到什麼話也說不出來，這樣的重逢真是可喜可賀。

「吉爾，你長得又高又壯！」奶奶說。

「梅蒂也是！看看她，頭髮多美，眼睛多漂亮！」爺爺說。

兄妹倆拍著手蹦呀跳呀，輪流撲到爺爺奶奶的懷抱裡。

過了很久，他們激動的情緒才稍稍平靜了一些。吉爾舒服地

坐在奶奶的膝上，梅蒂依偎在爺爺懷中，開始話起家常來了。

奶奶問：「爸爸和媽媽還好嗎？」

「很好，奶奶。我們出來的時候他們正睡得香呢。」吉爾回答說。

奶奶又親了親他們兩個。

「他們兩個多乾淨漂亮！多惹人喜愛！」奶奶誇獎說：「你們已經好幾個月沒來看我們了，怎麼不常來呢？忘了我們了嗎？我們在這裡一個人都見不到。」

「我們沒法來這裡呀！今天能來是多虧了仙女的幫忙。」吉爾說。

「我們總是待在這兒，天天盼望著世間的人來拜訪我們。」奶奶接著說，「上次你們來是在萬聖節那天。」

「萬聖節？可是那天我們沒出門呀，我們倆都感冒了！」

「一定是那天你們在懷念我們啦！每當你們想起我們時，我們就會醒來看見你們。」

吉爾明白了，爺爺奶奶並沒有完全離開，他的頭就靠在他日夜思念的奶奶的胸前！他問爺爺奶奶：「那麼你們真的沒有死嗎？」

倆老放聲大笑起來，自從他們離開人世過著這種美好舒適的生活，他們早已忘了「死」這個詞。於是爺爺問：「『死』這個詞是什麼意思？」

吉爾回答說：「『死』就是不再活著。」

爺爺和奶奶聳了聳肩膀。

「多麼荒謬啊，他們這些活著的人竟然如此認定不在世間的人！」

吉爾從爺爺的膝蓋上跳下來，四處東摸摸、西碰碰，每一個角落都不放過。他高興地發現，這裡的東西都是他十分熟悉的。

「一切還是原來的樣子，」他叫了起來「都還放在老地方！」很久沒來爺爺奶奶的家了，他覺得所有的東西都顯得比以前更美了。於是他又補充說：「這些東西都比以前更好看了。你看那座鐘！那個最長的指針的尖端就是被我給弄斷的。還有這鐘門上的小洞，也是我拿爺爺的搖鑽給鑽的呢。」

「沒錯！」爺爺說：「那時好多東西都被你弄壞了。那邊不就是你最喜歡爬的李樹嘛，只要我一不留神，你就爬上去了！」

「那隻青鳥是不是在這裡？」聊天之中，吉爾並沒忘記此行的目的。

梅蒂這時才抬頭，看見了一個鳥籠子。

「那不是老畫眉嗎？牠還唱歌嗎？」梅蒂叫道。

她的話音剛落，老畫眉就醒了，打開嗓子放聲歌唱起來。

「看到了吧，只要有人想念牠……」奶奶說。

這一切，讓吉爾驚訝不已。「牠是青色的！」吉爾喊了起來：「那隻鳥是青色的！像青色玻璃球一樣的青，嘿！就是這隻青鳥！你可以送給我嗎？」

爺爺和奶奶欣然同意了，吉爾拿起他剛放在樹下的鳥籠子，喜出望外且小心翼翼地把那隻寶貝鳥兒放進籠子裡。那鳥就在新籠子裡跳來跳去。

　　吉爾心裡甜滋滋的：「青鳥到手了，仙女見了會有多麼高興呀！光仙子也會很高興的。」

　　兄妹倆突然問起死去的兄弟姊妹們是否也在這裡。剎那間，兄弟姊妹總共七人發瘋似地跑到院子裡，原來他們一直在屋裡睡大覺。吉爾和梅蒂也迎了上去。他們擠作一團，然後興高采烈地互相擁抱著、跳著、轉著，歡樂地叫個不停。

　　「他們都在！他們都在！一提到他們，他們就都來了！」奶奶說：「這些小淘氣鬼！」

　　「哈哈！皮埃羅，我們又該像過去一樣較量一番了吧！」吉爾揪住了一個弟弟的頭髮「還有你，羅伯特。我說，瓊，你的陀螺怎麼樣啦？喂！美德蘭、皮蘭特、寶琳！啊，還有里凱特！」

　　「里凱特還沒學會走路！」梅蒂笑著說，「還在地上爬呢！」

　　吉爾發現一隻小狗在他們的周圍汪汪地狂叫。「這不是基基嘛？一點也沒變，牠的尾巴還是我用寶琳的剪刀修剪的呢。」

　　「說得對，這裡的一切都是不會變化的。」爺爺語重心長地說。

　　突然他們聽到屋裡的時鐘敲了八下。皆大歡喜的氣氛一下子沈寂下來，爺爺奶奶突然呆住了。「怎麼回事？」爺爺問奶奶，「這些天這口鐘從來不報時呀！剛才誰想到時間了？」奶奶回答說。

　　「是我，現在已經八點了！我和梅蒂必須走了！」吉爾說。「因為我們答應光仙子九點以前必須回去。」

吉爾說完就走向鳥籠子，但是大家正說得高興，都不願意他們這麼快就離開，這麼快就告別太掃興了！奶奶知道吉爾嘴饞，於是說他運氣真好，碰巧家裡有一些美味的白菜湯和李子餡餅。

　　「好吧。反正青鳥已經找到了。再說白菜湯可不是每天都能喝到的。」吉爾說。

　　孩子們趕忙把桌子搬到戶外，鋪好潔白的餐巾，擺好盤子。奶奶端來了湯碗，裡面盛著的白菜湯還熱氣騰騰。爺爺奶奶點亮了燈，和孫子、孫女們坐下來共進晚餐。一時間他們推推讓讓，說說笑笑。除了勺子盤子叮噹作響之外，別的什麼聲音也聽不見了。

　　吉爾貪婪地吃著：「真好吃！味道太美了！再來一些！再來一些！我還要一盤！」

　　「喂，當心點！安靜一點！瞧你這副吃相，和從前一模一樣！」爺爺說，「別把盤子弄破了！」

　　吉爾壓根兒不理爺爺的話，他站在凳子上，抓住湯鍋使勁往自己身邊拉。湯盆一歪，滾燙的菜湯灑得滿桌都是，滴到每一個人的腿上。孩子們都被燙得哇哇直叫。奶奶手忙腳亂，爺爺怒氣沖沖，打給了吉爾一個耳光。

　　吉爾先是一愣，然後捂著臉驚喜地叫著說：「打得好！爺爺，您的這一下子和從前活著的時候一樣有力！我真該吻您一下！」

　　大家全讓他逗笑了。

　　「要是你願意挨打，我可有的是勁兒！」爺爺繃起臉說。但

是爺爺很感動，他轉過臉去悄悄抹去了淚水。

「天哪！八點半了！」吉爾猛地站了起來說，「妹妹，我們得走了！」

奶奶懇求他們再待幾分鐘，但是沒辦法。

吉爾堅決地說：「不，不能再待了。我答應了仙子！」他趕快提起那個珍貴的鳥籠。

「再見了，爺爺……奶奶！兄弟姊妹們再見了！皮埃羅、羅伯特、寶琳、美德蘭、里凱特，還有你，小狗基基，我們再見了！我們不能再待了。別哭了，奶奶，我們會常來看你們的！」

奶奶說：「天天都來！這是我們唯一的快樂。只要經常想到來看我們，就是對我們最好的孝敬。」

兄弟姊妹們一起和他們道別：「再見！再見！早些來看我們！帶些大麥棒棒糖來給我們！」

他們對吉爾和梅蒂吻了又吻、親了又親，一起揮動著手帕高喊著告別的話。但是他們的聲音再也聽不見了，身影慢慢地消失了。濃霧又包圍了吉爾和梅蒂，遮天蔽日的古樹，又將他們籠罩在黑暗中。

「拉著我，哥哥！我好害怕！」梅蒂嗚嗚地哭了。

吉爾也渾身顫抖，但他有責任安慰妹妹。

吉爾說：「噓！別哭！別忘了，我們已帶回了青鳥！」

正說著，一線光亮劃破了林中的黑暗。吉爾手裡緊緊地握著鳥籠子，連忙走到光亮處。他借著這光亮一看，糟了！懷念國的那隻美麗的青鳥竟變成黑的了！不管他怎樣細看，仍然是一隻黑

色的畫眉。這隻老畫眉他再熟悉不過了，以前牠天天在門口的柳條籠子裡給他唱歌。這是怎麼回事？多令人痛心！這對他們來說似乎太殘忍了！

更倒楣的是，他再也找不到來時走過的那條路了，地上一朵朵白色的紫羅蘭也不見了。吉爾哭了起來。

幸好仙女曾答應過讓光仙子來照顧他們。迷霧突然再次散去，但是在他們面前出現的，不是爺爺奶奶的屋子，而是一座奇異的聖堂，聖堂中射出耀眼的光芒。

光仙子美麗又端莊地站在聖堂門口，穿著閃閃發光的衣服。她笑眯眯地聽著吉爾講述他的挫折，她洞悉一切，因為光包容一切，將愛灑向萬物。但是不曾有一個生靈毫無保留地接受光，熱愛光，所以也就沒人能領悟真理的奧秘。

「別難過。」光仙子對兄妹倆說，「難道見到了爺爺奶奶，你們還不高興嗎？難道有這樣的幸福，你們還不滿足嗎？你們讓那隻老畫眉獲得了新生，難道不因此感到愉快嗎？聽！畫眉在唱歌呢！」

老畫眉在籠子裡跳來跳去，盡情地唱著，黃色的小眼睛閃耀著歡快的光芒。

「親愛的孩子，在尋找青鳥的時候，你們也要學會愛護路上找到的灰鳥或黑鳥呀！」

美麗的光仙子很清楚青鳥在哪裡，但若是她告訴兩個孩子去哪兒找青鳥，那他們就會永遠也找不到牠了。在光仙子的精心照顧下，兄妹倆躺在美麗的白雲上進入了夢鄉。

第 4 章

夜之宮

　　天剛亮，大家準備到夜宮去，希望能在那找到青鳥。牛奶小姐和水姑娘都找了藉口請假；至於光仙子更不能去夜宮，因為她始終與黑夜不和；火是光的親戚，火先生當然也不喜歡黑夜。光仙子告訴狗先生蒂魯通往夜宮的道路，因為這次探險隊要由狗先生帶路。光仙子吻別了孩子們，這隻小小的隊伍就出發了。

　　蒂魯直立著身體像人一樣用後腿走路，搖搖擺擺地走在最前面。他從來沒顧慮過如果找到了青鳥，就意味著自己的生命即將結束，他盲目地加入了兩位小主人的行列尋找青鳥。「如果抓到那隻淘氣的青鳥，哪怕牠的味道跟鵪鶉一樣鮮美，我都不能舔牠一下，更別說嘗牠了！」

　　在狗先生後面的是麵包先生，他提著鳥籠一本正經地跑著，然後是吉爾和梅蒂，糖先生走在最後。

　　狡猾的貓女士哪兒去了？

　　「這些白癡！差點兒壞了我的大事，看來我只能靠自己了。」貓女士心想著，她決定趁天未亮前去拜會她的老朋友夜神。

　　貓女士飛也似的跑著，輕巧得像一片羽毛，身上披的斗篷被風鼓起，如同一面旗幟飄在身後；帽子上的羽飾有節奏地抖動著；腳下那雙灰色的羊皮靴簡直未曾碰地。她三竄兩跳，很快就到達了夜神居住的大廳，見到了夜神。

夜神像女王一樣威風凜凜地倚在寶座上睡著了。這裡的景象十分奇特，四周見不到一丁點兒亮光，連一顆小星星也沒有。但貓的眼睛能透視黑暗，所以對於貓女士來說，夜神不存在任何秘密。在她眼中，夜宮一覽無遺，如同置身於光天化日之下。

在夜神醒來之前，貓女士滿懷深情地看著夜神那張熟悉的臉。這張面孔神情冷漠、令人敬畏，如同月亮一樣呈銀白色，在長長的黑色輕紗下隱約可見夜神的軀體，體態如同希臘塑像一樣美麗。她長了一對翅膀，沒有胳膊，在熟睡之中巨大的翅膀收攏在兩側，使她看起來十分威嚴。

「夜神，是我，我累壞了。」

夜神的美建立在寧靜與安祥之上。她的本性多慮、極易恐慌，樹葉飄落、星星下墜、貓頭鷹鳴叫，甚至任何微不足道的小動靜，都足以撕裂她那每晚籠罩在大地上的黑色絨幕。她拍了拍巨大的翅膀，用顫抖的聲音問貓女士出了什麼事。什麼？有人要闖入她的宮殿裡！而且還要借助有魔力的鑽石揭開她的秘密！

「我看只有一個辦法，夜神。青鳥和月宮裡的鳥兒都關在大廳後面的大門裡，因此我們應該嚇唬嚇唬這些小孩子，讓他們不敢打開那扇大門。而其他門洞裡的奧秘，一定能把他們嚇個半死。我們能不能安全脫險，就看您能不能嚇住他們啦。」貓女士向夜神解釋她的對策。

除此之外沒有別的辦法了。夜神還來不及回答，就已經聽到

了腳步聲。只見她緊鎖著眉頭，氣憤地展開那雙翅膀。透過夜神的神情，貓女士知道她已同意了自己的計劃。

「他們來了！」貓女士叫起來。

一小隊人馬正走下陰森的夜宮臺階。巨大而奇特的黑色大理石宮殿，陰森森的像座墳墓，宮殿是圓的，四周烏黑的柱子聳向天空，看不見屋頂，只有抬頭仰望才能看到星星發射出來的微弱亮光。黑暗籠罩著每個角落，只有一左一右兩點火光在夜神的寶座兩側時隱時現地閃爍著。一個巨大的黃銅大門立在寶座後面，左右兩側的柱子之間露出幾個青銅大門。

貓女士迎向孩子們。「小主人！這邊走，我已經向夜神通報了，她很樂意見你們。請往這邊來。」吉爾勇敢而堅定地走向夜神的寶座，然後彬彬有禮地請求她允許在夜宮裡尋找青鳥。

「這裡沒有青鳥！我從來沒見過什麼青鳥。」夜神大喊起來，鼓動她那對巨大的翅膀嚇唬吉爾。

吉爾面無懼色，再三請求。夜神對他帽子上的那顆鑽石感到害怕，因為鑽石的光芒能驅逐黑暗，破壞她的權力。夜神想：還是裝作大發慈悲讓步比較妥當，於是她指著放在寶座前面臺階上的一把大鑰匙。

吉爾拿起鑰匙，毫不遲疑地向大廳裡的第一個門跑去。

其餘的幾位都嚇得渾身哆嗦。吉爾雖然也很害怕，卻還是堅定地要把門打開。夜神嚴厲的聲音壓倒所有的嘈雜聲，語氣很是嚇人：「裡面有鬼！」

狗先生蒂魯最恨妖魔鬼怪這一套了，他忠心耿耿守在吉爾身

旁，氣呼呼地喘著氣。

　　咔嚓一聲，鎖終於被打開了，大家屏住呼吸誰也不敢喘氣。霎時間，黑暗中影影綽綽出現一群白色的身影，向四面八方到處亂鑽。有的身影繞著柱子，有的拉長伸向天空，有的在地面上飛快地蜿蜒蠕動。它們的動作太快，難以看清它們的相貌，吉爾正拚命地驅趕著它們。夜神裝作嚇得要命，事實上，鬼一直是夜神的朋友，她一句話就能把這群鬼趕回原處。不過夜神反而瘋了似地拍打著翅膀，大呼小叫：「救命呀！救命呀！快趕走它們！快趕走它們！」

　　由於近年來沒人迷信鬼了，這些可憐的鬼難得有機會出來放放風，豈肯輕易回去！但是蒂魯一個勁兒地咬它們的腿，它們嚇得不敢久留，只好乖乖地回去。

　　鬼門終於關好了，狗先生這才舒了一口氣：「哼！誰不知道我的牙齒很鋒利，它們的腿咬起來就像棉花一樣！」

　　「這裡關的是什麼？」吉爾又向第二個門走去。「開這扇門要小心點兒嗎？」

　　「不用，大可不必小心。」夜神說，「裡面關的是病魔，這些可憐的小傢伙十分安靜，因為人類一直在向病魔開戰。打開門自己看吧。」

　　吉爾把門打開，裡面什麼也沒看到，正打算把門關上，一個戴著棉帽、穿著睡衣的小傢伙把他擠到一旁走出來。出來後，小東西在大廳裡跳來跳去，搖頭晃腦，不時地停下來咳嗽，又打噴嚏，又擤鼻涕。她穿的拖鞋太大，一路拖著走。吉爾和糖先生、

麵包先生不再害怕了，大笑了起來。可是沒等他們走近那戴棉布睡帽的小人兒，他們也開始咳嗽、打噴嚏。

夜神說：「這是感冒，微不足道的病魔。」

「我的老天爺！如果我的鼻子成天流鼻涕，我就完了！」糖先生暗暗叫苦：「我會融化的。」可憐的糖先生不知該躲到哪裡，他差點兒逃出夜宮，還好蒂魯及時趕來，在吉爾和梅蒂的笑聲中將那個鬼丫頭趕到了她的洞穴中。到目前為止，吉爾和梅蒂經歷的磨難並不太可怕，他們心中也就輕鬆起來。

因此吉爾向下一個門跑去，他的膽子更大了。

「當心！這裡關的是戰爭魔鬼！」夜神的聲音有些恐怖，「要是跑出來一個，後果不堪設想，它們的威力比往常任何時候都要大！你們都要站穩，做好把門關上的準備！」

夜神警告的話還沒說完，大膽的吉爾已經後悔自己太莽撞了。他還來不及把剛打開的門關上，一股不可抗拒的力量從門裡猛往外頂了出來，血像決口似地從門縫裡瀉出。戰火四下瀰漫，槍炮聲、喊殺聲、詛咒聲、呻吟聲交織在一起。夜宮裡一片混亂，人們四下奔逃，麵包先生和糖先生想逃又找不到出口，只好跑到吉爾身旁，拚命地用肩膀關門。

貓女士心裡高興卻假作慌張，她捋著觸鬚說：「這回他們一定不敢開下一個門了，該罷手了吧！」

蒂魯奮力幫助他的小主人，表現得像個超人一樣，而梅蒂站在一旁嚇得直哭。

最後，吉爾發出勝利的呼聲：「太好了！門又關上了！它們投降啦！我們勝利啦！」說著吉爾精疲力竭地坐在臺階上，渾身沒有一點兒力氣，他用嚇得瑟瑟發抖的小手，擦著額頭上的汗水。

夜神冷冷地問：「怎麼樣？吃夠了苦頭吧？看到戰爭魔鬼了吧！」

「看到了！看到了！」小吉爾抽抽噎噎地說：「太可怕了！它們太凶殘了，我想青鳥不可能會在那裡。」

「那是肯定的！」夜神很不愉快地說：「就算青鳥和它們在一起，也早被它們吃了！根本沒辦法找到青鳥，明白了吧！」

但是吉爾滿懷信心地站著，大聲說：「我要看看所有的地方，是光仙子這樣告訴我的！」

夜神反駁說：「說得可真容易，她自己卻躲在家裡不敢露面！」

「把下一道門打開」吉爾很堅定「讓我們看看裡面是什麼。」

「不能開那道門！」夜神心裡有鬼，厲聲地說。

「爲什麼呢？」

「因爲不容許打開這門！」

「那麼，青鳥就藏在裡面了！」

「不要開那道門！別往前走了！別拿性命開玩笑！」

但是吉爾固執地又問：「這究竟是爲什麼呀？」

吉爾一定要弄明白眞相，一下子便惹惱了夜神。她勃然大怒地使出了最後一招來嚇唬吉爾：

 青鳥

「凡是打開那扇門的，都休想重見天日！那就是意味著開門者必死無疑！你們見到過的最可怕的情景，跟它們比起來都不算什麼，如果你堅持要開那扇門，它們正等著你呢！」

麵包先生牙齒抖個不停地央求說：「親愛的主人！可憐可憐我們吧！別去開那道門，別去開門！我跪下來求您了！」

貓女士也極力表示反對：「你這是在用我們的生命做代價！」

「我不要你去！我不要你去！」梅蒂抽噎著說。

糖先生合攏十指哭著說：「行行好吧！行行好吧！」

小伙伴們都圍在他身邊哭著求他，只有蒂魯沒反抗主人的意願。雖然他也知道最後時刻即將來到，即便兩行熱淚流下面頰他也沒吭聲。他舔了舔吉爾的手，十分絕望。由於極度痛苦，吉爾的心狂跳著，猶豫不決，他不願在可憐的小伙伴面前表現出自己的軟弱無能，他想：「如果讓我的伙伴們看到我無能為力，我就徹底完蛋了，如果我表現得軟弱無能，不能完成任務，誰還去執行這個任務？我就永遠無法找到青鳥了。」

吉爾決心犧牲自己。他揮動手中的金鑰匙大聲說：「我一定要打開這道門！」

他帶著氣喘吁吁的蒂魯跑向那道大門。這位可憐的狗先生，他的自尊心以及對吉爾的忠誠壓倒了恐懼。於是他對主人說：「我不怕，我留下！我要和我的小主人待在一起！」

其餘的幾位這時都躲起來了。麵包先生躲在柱子後面抖個不停；糖先生躲在角落裡，癱軟在地上，抱著梅蒂不斷融化著；夜

神和貓女士在大廳的另一端遠遠地觀望著，氣得渾身發抖。

　　吉爾把蒂魯摟到胸口緊緊擁抱著，又吻了吻他。他將鑰匙插進鎖孔，手不顫、臂不抖，小伙伴們則嚇得躲在角落裡尖叫起來。只見大門在吉爾面前神奇地開了。真是令人喜出望外！眼前的情景令吉爾又驚又喜、目瞪口呆，在他面前出現的是一個夢幻般的花園。在這個夢幻般的花園裡，瀑布從天而降，花朵閃閃發光，樹木披著銀色的月光；一群東西在一簇簇玫瑰之間飛來飛去，像藍色的雲彩。吉爾真不敢相信眼前的情景是真的，他擦了擦眼睛，定了定神，又仔細看看，然後衝進花園發了瘋一樣地喊：

　　「我們終於找到了！成千上萬隻青鳥！快來呀！快呀！成千上萬隻青鳥，牠們在這裡！梅蒂和蒂魯，快來呀！你們都快來看呀！來幫我捉呀！牠們多得伸手就能抓住好幾隻呢！快過來幫我！」對眼前發生的事確信無疑之後，他的朋友們全都飛也似地奔過來，衝到鳥群中捉鳥，比賽看誰捉得最多。

　　梅蒂喊道：「我捉住七隻了！太多了，沒辦法拿！」

　　「我也沒辦法再拿了，你看，我捉了這麼多了！牠們從我的懷裡飛掉了！」

青鳥

吉爾說，「蒂魯也捉到了幾隻。我們出去吧！快走吧！光仙子正等著我們，她一定會很高興的。從這邊走！這邊！」

他們蹦蹦跳跳，唱著勝利之歌，歡天喜地地從夜宮出來了。

夜神和貓沒有分享他們的歡樂，她們憂心忡忡地站在大門前。夜神哭著問：「青鳥被他們捉住了嗎？」

「沒有。」貓女士回答說。她看到那隻真正的青鳥，高高地棲息在月亮射出來的光線上。「牠飛得太高了，他們捉不到牠。」

吉爾和他的朋友們飛快地爬上通向陽光的無數層臺階，每個人都高高興興、急急忙忙，懷裡緊緊地抱著自己捉來的鳥。可是當他們沿著臺階來到陽光下的時候，懷中的鳥全都死了。

光仙子正焦急地等著他們。「怎麼樣！抓到青鳥了嗎？」

吉爾高興地說：「抓到了！抓到了！青鳥可真多呀！您看，有好幾千隻呢，成千上萬！」

說完，他大驚失色，只見這些可憐的鳥翅膀都折斷了，腦袋無力地垂在脖子上。吉爾回頭看著他的伙伴們。多慘！他們抱著的也是一堆死鳥！

吉爾痛哭著撲到光仙子的懷裡。他的希望再一次成為了泡影。

「孩子，別哭！」光仙子勸他說，「你們沒有捉到能在陽光下活著的那隻青鳥，不過……我們一定能找到牠的。」

麵包先生和糖先生幾乎異口同聲地說：「我們一定會找到牠！」他們以此來安慰吉爾。蒂魯對眼前的情景有點不知所措，望著這些死鳥，他竟然一時忘了尊嚴，脫口說：「這些鳥肉不知好不好吃？」

他們都動身到光仙子的聖堂裡去，要在那裡過夜。

糖先生湊到麵包先生身邊，壓低聲音對他說：「主席先生，您不認為我們這樣四處跑來跑去是在白費力氣嗎？」

受到糖先生這樣的奉承，麵包先生感到飄飄然了。他自命不凡地說：「我親愛的夥計，不用擔心。如果我們老是任憑那個冒失鬼異想天開瞎折騰，還有誰能活得下去！明天我們就賴在床上！」

最後，光仙子的聖堂聳立在水晶嶺上，不斷地閃著耀眼的光芒。疲乏的孩子讓蒂魯輪流背負著他們，抵達那閃亮的階梯時，孩子們幾乎都睡著了。

第 5 章
未來王國

　　所有動物和靜物都聚集在光仙子聖堂的地下室裡，光仙子認為不能放任他們自由，不然他們准會逃出去惹是生非。地下洞穴有沙發和黃金餐桌，光仙子的僕人還在餐桌上擺放好水果、奶油蛋糕和美酒。動物和靜物們很樂意待在這兒，吃喝和睡覺是他們最喜歡的事了。除了蒂魯，但光仙子對他說，以後孩子們還會經歷另一場考驗，屆時他能協助孩子們。

　　說完，光仙子用仙杖碰了碰翡翠牆，翡翠牆馬上分開了，然後她帶著孩子們穿牆而過，離開了地下洞穴。

　　光仙子的車子在聖堂外等候，車上鑲著黃金碧玉，漂亮極了。他們上了車坐好，繫在車前的兩隻白鳥立刻展翅高飛，拉著車子直上雲霄。那車子的速度極快，吉爾和梅蒂樂得手舞足蹈。

四周的雲彩慢慢消失了，他們突然發現自己站在一個富麗堂皇、瓊樓玉宇般的宮殿中。眼前的一切都是青色的：光亮的石板路、柱子、穹隆狀屋頂，甚至宮殿裡最細小的東西也全都是青色的。宮殿一望無際，放眼只見浩瀚無涯的一片碧綠，讓人覺得如臨仙境。

　　吉爾不禁讚歎道：「天哪！真是太美了！我們是在什麼地方呢？」

　　「我們在未來王國。」光仙子說：「來到了還未出世的孩子們所待的地方。說不定在這裡我們還能找到青鳥。看，孩子們跑過來了！」

青鳥

　　一群群孩子從四面八方跑過來，他們從頭到腳都穿戴成青色，個個美麗無比，有人黑髮、有人金髮，他們興高采烈地喊著：「快來看喲！出生後的孩子來了！」

　　「這麼多孩子！這麼多呀！」吉爾嚷道。

　　「還有更多呢！」光仙子說，「沒有誰能數得清楚。再往前走走，你還會看到很多東西呢。」

　　吉爾按光仙子說的使勁往前擠，可是他幾乎是寸步難移。他們身邊已經擠滿了身穿青色衣服的孩子，要擠出一條路往前走可真不容易。吉爾終於爬上了一個臺階，這才使目光越過密密麻麻的腦袋，看清楚整個宮殿裡其他地方的情景。真是奇特！吉爾高興地跳起來，就是做夢也夢不到這樣的場面！梅蒂跟在他身後，踮起腳尖看著，不停地拍手叫絕。

　　周圍有成千上萬個穿青色衣服的孩子。他們有的在四處走動，有的在玩耍，有一些在說話或在沉思，有一些在睡覺，還有些在工作。和宮殿的主色調一樣，他們用的工具、製造的機器，以及他們栽種的樹木或是採集的果子和花朵，一律都是青色。

　　有一個青衣小孩子站在吉爾身邊，他個子很小，青色的衣襟下露出一雙胖呼呼的小腳丫。他好奇地凝視著吉爾，不由自主地向他走來。

　　「你好！」吉爾把手向青衣小孩伸去。

　　但是青衣小孩在那裡站著沒有反應，他不懂吉爾伸出手來是什麼意思。

　　小孩聚精會神地看著吉爾，並伸出手指一本正經地碰了碰吉爾的帽子，咬著舌頭口齒不清地問：

「這是什麼呀？」

吉爾回答說：「這是我的帽子呀！你沒有帽子嗎？」

「沒有，那是做什麼用的呀？」小孩問。

「問候人時要用它致意，天冷時要把它戴上。」吉爾回答道。

「『天冷』是什麼意思？」小孩又問。

「當你凍得直打哆嗦，就是『冷』呀，就像這個樣子！」吉爾做出打哆嗦的樣子給他看。「或者是這樣。」吉爾裝成很冷又使勁兒地搓著手。

「地球上很冷嗎？」小孩問。

「是的，如果在冬天沒有火爐時是很冷的。」

「為什麼沒有火爐呢？」

「因為生火爐很花錢，木柴是要花錢買來的呀。」

那孩子又打量了吉爾一番，彷彿他一句也沒聽懂吉爾的話似的。吉爾也覺得迷惑不解。

「你多大了？」吉爾問他。

「快要出生了，還要過十二年。」青衣小孩說：「出生好玩嗎？」

「哦，是的。好玩極了！」吉爾不假思索地回答。

「聽說你們那裡很有趣，已出生的人們也都很可愛。」青衣小孩子說。

「對呀，是很不錯。」吉爾說：「那裡有鳥，有玩具，還有

蛋糕。有的孩子三樣都有。要是一樣也沒有的人，可以看別人的。」

吉爾雖然自己很貧窮，卻沒感到痛苦，而是為別人的富有高興。

兩個孩子聊了很長的時間，就在這時候，他感到背後吹來了一陣風。他扭過頭，看見離他不遠處有一台大機器。機器非常雄偉壯觀，但還沒有名字，因為未來王國裡的創造發明，必須等到它們在世間出現時，才會由人類來命名。看著這台機器，吉爾心想：眼前那飛也似旋轉的青色大翅膀，像極了自己見過的風車的葉片。要是找到了青鳥，牠的翅膀也不見得會比這個精緻、好看了。他驚歎不已地問他的新朋友：這玩意兒究竟是什麼。

「你說那個東西？那是我將在人世間創造發明的東西的。」

見吉爾瞪著眼睛還沒有明白，小孩又補充說：「等我到人世間後，我就要發明創造給人們帶來幸福的東西。你想看一看嗎？它就在那兩根柱子中間。」

吉爾轉身過去，沒想到所有的青衣小孩都喊叫著一擁而上：

「不！先過來看我的吧！」

「不！我的比他的還要好！」

「我的發明更了不起！」

「看看我用糖做的機器。」

「他做的不好！」

「我帶來一種誰也沒見過的光！」說完，青衣小孩全身點燃了最耀眼的一圈火焰。

在一片歡樂聲中,吉爾和梅蒂被青衣孩子們簇擁到青色工廠裡。小發明家們紛紛開動了自己的機器。有的機器從地面掠過;有的則沖上了房頂。這些機器是由一種能旋轉的裝置提供動力,裝置是用圓盤、皮帶、滑輪、主動輪、齒輪、螺旋槳構成的。那些青衣孩子們有的展開自己的藍圖,有的翻開巨大的書籍,有的揭開青色雕像的蓋布,有的則拿出彷彿是用藍寶石和綠松石製成的碩大的花朵和果實。

吉爾和梅蒂看得目瞪口呆,不停地拍手叫絕,好像置身在天堂一般。梅蒂笑著俯下身去,把頭伸到一朵巨花的花瓣中。花瓣如同青色綢緞頭巾,將梅蒂的頭圍起來。一個長著一頭烏黑的頭髮和一對深邃大眼睛的漂亮孩子,扶著花莖驕傲地說:「等我出生以後,花都要開這麼大!」

這時，另一位小男孩，在一個高個子幫助下，提著一隻大柳條籃子走了過來，小男孩幾乎被大籃子擋住了。籃子邊垂下的綠葉底下，一個長著金黃色頭髮、紅潤臉蛋兒的小孩對著吉爾笑著叫道：

「看哪，我的蘋果多麼大！」

「那是西瓜嘛！」吉爾叫起來。

「不！不是西瓜！是我的蘋果！」青衣小孩說：「等我出世後，所有的蘋果都會這麼大！我發現了新的栽植方法！」

吉爾抓緊時間儘量多結識一些孩子。他認識了新太陽的發現者、為大家謀福利的創造者、剷除人世間不平的英雄，以及將要戰勝死亡的小菁英……要認識的孩子太多了！吉爾正累得精疲力竭，招架不住時，一個小孩的聲音引起了他的注意：

「吉爾！吉爾！真是你嗎？你好嗎？」

一個青衣小孩從大廳後面跑過來，一路推開人群。他細高的個子，白白的皮膚，一雙明亮的大眼睛，看起來真像梅蒂。

「你怎麼會知道我的名字？」吉爾訝異地問。

青衣小孩說：「這有什麼，我是你未來的弟弟呀！」

吉爾和梅蒂驚訝得目瞪口呆！能見到未來的弟弟太不尋常了！回家一定要告訴爸爸、媽媽，他們要是聽到這樣的消息一定會大吃一驚的！

那個小孩繼續解釋說：「明年我就會出生，那是復活節之前的星期天。」

接著，他又向未來的哥哥問了一連串的問題：家裡舒服嗎？

飯菜好不好吃？爸爸媽媽的脾氣怎樣？

「哦！媽媽非常慈祥！」梅蒂對她尚未出生的弟弟說。

接著吉爾和梅蒂又問那個小孩一些問題。他要在人世間做什麼？他會帶來什麼？

「我帶的是疾病：猩紅熱、百日咳還有麻疹。」他們未來的小弟弟說。

「噢！為什麼？」吉爾驚叫著，大惑不解地搖了搖頭。

小孩接著說：「然後我就會離開你們。」

「你這樣子來去匆匆真是太不值得了！」吉爾心裡很難過，不大高興地說。

「可是我也沒有辦法呀！」小弟弟也有點惱火。

不等小弟弟出世，這哥倆就幾乎要吵起來！這時一群青衣小孩突然一窩蜂地擠著，好像是忙著去迎接什麼人，把兩人阻隔開了。同時，一陣軋軋聲響起，彷彿長廊上有成千上萬扇無形的門同被打開。

「怎麼啦？」吉爾問。

「是『時間』來了。」一個小孩說：「他正在開門呢。」

大廳裡一下子騷動起來。孩子們丟下機器和手邊的工作，睡著的也醒了，大家都急切地盯著大廳後面乳白色的門，嘴裡不停地念著「時間老人」；到處都能聽到這樣的呼喚聲。神秘的開門聲依舊在大廳中持續著。吉爾急於知道真相，他抓住了一個小孩的衣襟，向他打聽究竟發生了什麼事。

「放開我。」那孩子焦急地說：「我急死了，今天也許會輪

到我！天已破曉了，正是今天該出生的孩子們動身到世間的時刻，你會看到的，『時間』老人拔起門閂了。」

「誰是『時間老人』？」吉爾問。

「就是安排要出生的孩子們動身的那位老人。」另一個小孩說：「他人不算壞，只是不講情面，如果還沒輪到你，不論怎樣求他，他都會把你推開，休想矇混過關。就要輪到我了，也該輪到我了。」

突然光仙子驚慌失措地趕到吉爾和梅蒂面前。

「快走！我正到處找你們呢！千萬別讓『時間老人』看到你們！」

說完光仙子用她那金色的斗篷裹著兩個孩子，然後將他們拉到了角落裡。在這裡，他們能清楚地看到發生的一切，但是不會被發現。

受到光仙子的保護，吉爾鬆了一口氣。現在他明白了，即將出現在他眼前的這個人，威力無比，凡人是無法與他對抗的。他既是神又是妖怪，他賜予生命又吞噬生命；他速度極快，匆匆地從世上掠過，世人們都來不及見其真面目，他不停地吞噬著生命。在吉爾家裡，他已經擄走爺爺、奶奶、吉爾的兄弟姊妹，還有那隻老畫眉。他從不在乎所擄走的是什麼，不管是喜是悲，是冬是夏，都是他的囊中之物！

那麼，為什麼未來王國的孩子們還要爭先恐後地飛跑著去迎接他呢？吉爾對此感到迷惑。「也許在這裡他什麼也不吞噬！」吉爾這樣想。

那扇門緩緩開起,他來了!遠處響起了人世間的音樂聲!紅綠相映的光照亮了大廳。一位又高又瘦的老人邁進了門檻,他就是「時間老人」,他的臉上好像蒙上了一層灰塵,全是皺紋,衰老得如同變成了灰似的,長長的白鬍子一直垂至膝蓋。他一手拿著一把巨大的鐮刀,另一隻手拿一把銅壺滴漏。在他的身後,停著一艘豪華的大船,揚著白帆飄蕩在雲海上。

「時辰已到的人,準備好了沒有?」時間老人的聲音好像銅鐘一般莊嚴而又宏亮。他的話音未落,一片銀鈴般清脆的聲音從大廳裡響起:

「準備好了!準備好了!準備好了!」

霎時間,孩子們把高大的老頭子圍得水泄不通;時間老人把孩子們推到一邊,厲聲說:「一個一個來!又來這麼多,人數已遠遠超過了名額。你們是騙不了我的!」

他揮動著手中的大鐮刀,另一隻手同時扯開衣襟,擋住了冒冒失失的孩子們的去路,不讓他們矇混過關。老人神情嚴峻,沒有誰能逃過他尖銳的眼睛。

青鳥

「還沒輪到你！」他對一個孩子說，「你明天才能出生！也沒輪到你，你還得等好幾年！想成為第十三個牧羊人？有十二個就足夠了，已經太多了！什麼？想做醫生？已經太多了！世上的醫生們還在抱怨沒工作呢！有沒有想當工程師的？他們需要一個誠實的工程師。只一個，最出色的！」

決定孩子們去留的事繼續進行：被擋回去的孩子垂頭喪氣地繼續幹活，而被接納的人，便受到其餘人羨慕的目光。但偶爾也會有一些意外，例如那個想去戰勝不公平的小英雄緊拉著小伙伴們的手，不願意出生。小伙伴們為他央求時間老人：「他不肯去，大人！」

「我不去！」小傢伙拚命掙扎著，「我不想出生！」

「他的選擇沒錯！」吉爾想，他很明白人世間是怎麼一回事。不該失敗的人總是失敗、罪犯逍遙法外，被懲罰的卻是無辜的人們！

「要是我，也不會去投胎！我寧願天天去找青鳥！」吉爾自言自語道。

這時，那個正義小鬥士啜泣著走了，他被時間老人給嚇壞了。

此刻的場面熱鬧到了極點。孩子們都在大廳裡跑來跑去忙成一團，要動身的忙著收拾他們發明的東西。

時間老人揮動著他手中的大鑰匙和可怕的鐮刀，扯開嗓門大聲吼道：「船起錨了！」

於是將出世的孩子爬上掛著美麗白帆的金色大船，戀戀不捨地向留下來的朋友們揮手告別。可是當他們一看到遠處的人間大地，便高興地歡呼起來：「瞧！多明亮啊！」、「多麼廣闊啊！」

遠處響起了一陣歌聲。像從深淵中傳出來似的，那是遠方飽含著歡樂和期望的歌聲。

聽了這些歌聲，光仙子的臉上現出了微笑，她俯身告訴迷惑不解的吉爾：「這是媽媽們迎接孩子降生所唱的歌。」

這個時候，已經關上門的時間老人發現了吉爾和梅蒂。他勃然大怒，揮舞著鐮刀向他們衝了過來。

「快跑！快跑！」光仙子大聲喊道：「拿著青鳥，和梅蒂到我面前來！」

光仙子將事先藏在衣襟下的青鳥塞到吉爾懷中，邊跑邊展開她那耀眼的面紗，把孩子們罩在光幕下，保護著他們免受時間老人的殘害。

他們穿過好幾條雄偉壯觀的長廊，有青綠色的也有天藍色的，可是他們還是置身於時間老人的未來王國。由於觸怒了時間老人，他們必須儘快撤離。

梅蒂嚇壞了，吉爾則緊張不安地不斷回頭看著光仙子。

「別怕！」光仙子說：「你只要照顧好青鳥就可以了。這隻鳥顏色非常地青，美麗極了！」

吉爾一想起懷中的青鳥，就禁不住心花怒放。他能感到那隻寶貝鳥兒在他懷中撲啦啦地抖動翅膀。他不敢用力壓住鳥兒柔滑而溫暖的翅膀。他的心緊貼著青鳥的心，在怦怦地跳著。

　　他們剛要跨出宮殿的門檻，突然一陣強風掠過大廳，吹開了光仙子披在兄妹倆身上的面紗，讓時間老人看到了他們。時間老人怒吼著，揮起鐮刀砍向吉爾。吉爾嚇得大叫一聲，光仙子擋開砍過來的鐮刀，宮殿大門在他們身後砰一聲關上了。他們逃出來了！但是吉爾慌亂之中鬆開了雙臂，那隻未來王國之鳥在他的淚眼中飛越他們的頭頂，那雙翅膀如夢如幻，若有若無，很快消融在蔚藍色的天空中，直到吉爾再也辨認不出牠的輪廓了。

第 6 章
享樂宮

隔天早上，光仙子告訴兄妹倆，這次他們要前往享樂宮。

「我相信這次一定能找到青鳥。」

一行人走到一個十分典雅的大廳中。大廳裡裝飾得很美，洋溢著一種威尼斯和佛蘭芒文藝復興時期放縱、奢華的氣息。中間是一張氣派非凡、碧玉鑲嵌的大餐桌，上面擺放著金盤銀盞、玻璃杯、燭臺，還有各種精妙絕倫、賞心悅目的珍饈美味。世上最奢侈的享樂者們繞桌而坐，有的在吃、有的在喝、有的在唱、有的輾轉反側、有的舉酒乾杯、有的則懶散地閑坐著，還有的乾脆倒在糕點水果、佳肴美味和狼藉的杯盤之間睡著了。

他們一個個肥頭大耳、滿面紅光、衣著華麗、鑲金綴玉，一派珠光寶氣。妖豔的女僕不停地把誘人的菜餚

和醇香的美酒端上來，大廳中燈光通明，並且回響著俗不可耐、低級刺耳的樂聲。

　　見此光景，兄妹倆和他們的伙伴們十分驚恐，紛紛圍著光仙子。貓女士則不聲不響地來到大廳後面，從一道黑色的帷幔中消失了。

　　「這些胖子是什麼人？這麼快活，能吃這麼多好東西。」吉爾問光仙子。

　　光仙子回答說：「他們是最奢侈的享樂派。青鳥有時會誤入歧途來這裡，雖然可能性不太大。但現在你還不能轉動鑽石，我們要一步一步尋找青鳥，先從大廳的這邊開始。」

　　「可以靠近他們嗎？」

　　「當然可以！最奢侈的享樂派雖然粗俗沒教養，心眼還不壞。」

　　梅蒂瞧著那些糕點和糖果，讚歎著說：「多精美啊！」

　　「還有野味！羊腿！牛肝！香腸！」蒂魯也讚不絕口：「再也沒有什麼東西比牛肝更可口的了。」

　　這時，有十幾個最奢侈的享樂者站了起來，挺著大肚子搖晃著向孩子們走來。吉爾急忙退到光仙子的身邊。

　　「別怕！孩子們，他們很好客，很可能是過來請你們赴宴的！」光仙子安慰說：「不過你們什麼也別接受，這些糕點會破壞你們的意志，很危險！」

　　「什麼，一塊糕點也不能接受嗎？」吉爾很是不解「那些糕點多漂亮啊！還撒著一層糖霜！還有蜜餞和奶油！」

　　享樂派中最肥胖的一位向吉爾伸出手來說：「我是富翁享樂派——最奢侈的享樂派之一。我代表弟兄們請你們賞光，享用一下這些我們無法吃完的美味佳餚。」然後他緊拉著吉爾的手說：「宴會馬上又開始了。跟我過去吧，大家都在等你們呢！你沒聽到這些狂歡的人們叫喊著要你過去嗎？人太多了，我無法一一向你介紹。請讓我帶你們去貴賓席。」

　　「富翁享樂派先生，十分感謝。」吉爾說：「不過很遺憾，我們不能過去，我們正忙著找青鳥，現在沒時間。我想也許你會知道青鳥藏在哪裡？」

　　「青鳥？我想想。啊，對了，我想起來了。那種鳥的味道我想是不太鮮美。我們的餐桌上從來沒有青鳥，這也就是說我們不大看得上青鳥。」

　　「你們以什麼為生？」吉爾問。

　　「我們整天忙得無事可做。」富翁享樂派笑著說：「我們必須吃呀，喝呀，睡呀，忙得連休息的時間都沒有！」

　　「快樂嗎？」

「快樂，當然，快樂的生活必須是這個樣子。」富翁享樂派回答說：「除了這些，世上的生活還能有什麼呢？」

「你說的可是真心話？」光仙子問。

富翁享樂派覺得受了冒犯：「這個沒有教養的人是誰？」

吉爾看見自己的幾個同伴已經和享樂派們坐在一起了，如同親兄弟一般又吃又喝，縱情作樂。

「快看！他們開始吃了！」吉爾衝著光仙子喊。

光仙子指示吉爾說：「轉動鑽石！快，是時候了！」

吉爾一轉動鑽石，眼前的一切景物都變了。厚厚的紫紅帷幔、富麗堂皇的裝飾沒了，眼前呈現的是雄偉壯觀的大廳，彷彿身處在寧靜、清爽宜人的大教堂中，高大純白到幾近透明的建築裡，綿延無止盡的布簾高掛在無數個纖長潔淨的柱子上，十分和諧。縱情歡宴的餐桌已沒了蹤影，享樂派們的華麗衣冠變得支離破碎，脫落在腳下，和畫著笑臉的面具堆在一起。享樂派們大驚失色，繼而又垂頭喪氣，如同泄了氣的皮球，眨著眼對著不知從何處射來的的光線。直到現在他們才清楚自己的本來面目：赤身裸體、樣子臃腫醜陋，他們因羞愧絕望而驚叫著。

「天哪！」吉爾望著四下逃竄的享樂派，感歎著說：「他們怎麼會如此醜陋？他們會到哪裡去呢？」

「他們早已不知所措了，我想他們會去『痛苦』那裡避難。」光仙子說，「我擔心到那兒後他們永遠也無法解脫！」

望著眼前的景象，吉爾很吃驚：「這裡好美，我們到了哪兒？」

「我們並沒有動。」光仙子說：「不過是我們眼睛的視野改變了，現在所看到的是事物的本質。很快我們就會弄清楚哪些快樂能經受起鑽石光的照射。」

吉爾有些感慨：「太美了！瞧！有人過來要和我們說話。」

天使般的生靈在大廳裡出現了。他們彷彿剛從沈睡中甦醒，步履輕盈，體態優美，從柱子之間飄然而來。

「呀！這麼多！」吉爾大聲說：「他們從四面八方向這裡湧來！」

光仙子告訴他：「原先這樣的生靈還有很多，享樂派使他們受了極大的傷害。」

吉爾安慰說：「沒關係的，還有這麼多呢。」

一群小個子歡呼雀躍著跑出來圍著吉爾和梅蒂跳起舞來。

「太漂亮了！他們真漂亮！」吉爾讚不絕口「他們是誰，從哪兒來的？」

「是兒童們的幸福。」光仙子說。

又有一群高個子幸福跑進大廳。他們高聲地唱著歌。「在那兒！他們在那兒！」他們歡快地圍著吉爾和梅蒂跳起舞來。跳完後，一個領隊模

樣的人來到吉爾面前，並向他伸出手來。

　　「我是你們家的幸福領隊。這些是你們家庭其他的幸福成員。」

　　吉爾很難為情地問：「我們家中有幸福存在嗎？」家庭幸福成員們聽了都哈哈大笑。

　　「都聽到了吧！」他們大聲說道：「嘿，你這小傢伙，你們家的每個角落都充滿著幸福！我們唱呀，笑呀，創造的快樂都能撐破你家的房子！可是對我們所做的努力，你始終聽而不聞，視而不見。先做個自我介紹吧。我是身體健康幸福。能記住我嗎？不算最漂亮，但卻是最重要的。這位幾乎透明的是空氣清新幸福；這位穿著灰衣服的是愛戴父母幸福，由於從來沒人看他一眼，顯得有些憂傷；還有穿藍衣服的藍天幸福。穿綠衣的當然是樹林幸福了，在窗前就會看到他的；這位是陽光幸福，他的衣服像鑽石顏色；這位穿翡翠色衣服的是春天幸福。」

　　「你們每天都是這麼美麗嗎？」吉爾問。

　　身體健康幸福說：「當然。不論在哪個家庭，清晨人們醒來時，我們都打扮得如同過星期天。晚上最氣派的是日落幸福，世界上所有帝王的穿著都比不上他；星星幸福穿著金光閃爍的衣服跟在他身後，如同一位老神仙；天陰時有下雨幸福，渾身掛滿了珍珠；爐火幸福在冬天用他紫色的光熱溫暖冰冷的手；噢，最美好的幸福是無憂無慮幸福，你很快就能看到；在他們的眾兄弟之中，天真無邪幸福也算是一員，他是我們之中最晶瑩璀璨的；還有……」

「可是，太多了！這樣子是介紹不完的。而且我必須首先向那些偉大的喜悅報告，他們就在後面，靠近天堂之門，還沒有聽說你們的到來……讓我們最敏捷的在露水中奔跑的幸福去叫他們。」

「你們知道青鳥在哪裡嗎？」吉爾問。

家庭幸福領隊迷惑不解地說：「哈！他居然不知道青鳥在哪兒！」所有家庭幸福的成員都哈哈大笑。

吉爾有些生氣：「我就是不知道，這有什麼好笑的……」

「我們見過的最純潔的快樂就要到了。」家庭幸福領隊對吉爾說。

「她在哪兒？」吉爾問。

「難道你沒認出來嗎？睜開心靈之眼仔細看看！她是你母親的快樂呀！她已經看到你了！她向你跑來，將你摟在懷裡了！無與倫比的母愛快樂！」

見到母愛快樂，剛才從四下裡趕來的眾多快樂，全敬畏地退向一邊，讓出了一條路來。

母愛快樂大聲呼喚著：「吉爾！梅蒂！真沒想到在這裡能看見你們。待在家裡太孤單了，想不到你們都到天上來了！所有母親的靈魂都在歡快地微笑。你們倆快到我懷裡來！先讓我好好親親你們！親個夠！再也沒有比和你們在一起更幸福的了！」

吉爾結巴著說：「剛才我不知道妳是媽媽，妳看起來比往常漂亮多了！」

「當然了。因為我的青春不會消逝！你們每對我微笑一次，我就會年輕一年，每天都能給我帶來新的青春活力、新的幸福。」

吉爾非常驚訝。他發呆地望著她並吻著她：「太漂亮了！妳的衣服是用什麼做的？絲綢？珍珠？還是白銀？」

母愛快樂笑著說：「是用親吻、愛撫和慈愛的目光做成的。你們每親吻我一次，我的衣服就會增添一縷光彩。」

「眞有趣！沒想到媽媽這麼富有！從前妳把這麼美的衣服藏到哪兒了？是不是在只有爸爸才知道的衣櫃裡？」

「不是的。我一直穿著這件衣服，但沒有人能看見它，因爲人們的心靈之眼沒開時什麼也看不到。所有愛孩子的母親都是富有的，她們既不會貧窮醜陋，也不曾失去青春。是愛讓她們永遠享受最美好的快樂，哪怕是在悲傷的時候，她們只要親吻一下孩子，她們的淚珠就會變成星星掛在她們的眼睛深處。」

吉爾看著她的眼睛驚叫起來：「是眞的！妳的眼睛裡有好多好多星星呢，眞的是妳的眼睛，只是更美了……妳的雙手，還戴著那枚小戒指呢。手上妳點燈時燙到的傷痕還在，可是妳的手看起來晶瑩剔透，白淨細膩！眞怪，妳的聲音比在家時好聽多了……」

母愛耐心地說：「你們來到這裡，就一定要學會平時在家怎麼眞正看待我。吉爾明白了嗎？只要母親和孩子擁抱在一起，那裡就是天堂。每個孩子都只有一個母親，不可能有第二個，這位母親永遠是天下最美的。孩子應當盡力去理解自己的母親……不過你怎麼能找到這條路，怎麼會來到這裡？人類有史以來，就一

直在尋找這條路。」

　「是光仙子帶我來的。」吉爾指著光仙子。

　母愛快樂擁抱著光仙子：「你對我的孩子們眞是太好了！」

　光仙子說：「我將永遠善待那些相互愛戴的人們。」

　她們深深親吻了一下。然後她們抬起了頭，眼中滿是淚水。

　「你們爲什麼哭了？」吉爾看著所有的快樂驚訝地說：「你們都在哭！爲什麼呢？」

　光仙子溫柔地對他說：「噓！安靜點，我的孩子。」

第 7 章
墓地

當孩子們不出去探險的時候，就在光仙子的聖堂裡遊玩。這裡只有溫暖的夏天而沒有黑夜。時間是用不同色彩來分別的，有白時、粉時、黃時、紫時、綠時和藍時；花鳥、蝴蝶和水果的色彩和氣味都按不同時間的色調來變化，讓吉爾和梅蒂不斷感到驚奇。玩累了，就舒舒服服地躺在又長又寬如同小船的蜥蜴背上，由蜥蜴馱著走過花園裡的小路，越過沙灘。這裡的沙子又白又甜如同白糖一樣。要是渴了，水姑娘就對著杯子一樣的花朵輕輕一抖秀髮，花朵中就裝滿了水。吉爾和梅蒂就可以飲用這些百合、鬱金香、劍蘭花的花朵中的水；要是餓了，他們就吃樹上的水果，這些都是光仙子喜歡的水果，晶瑩透亮、味道奇特。

在一片灌木叢中，有一泓神奇的池水。池水清澈如鏡，面對著池水，從水裡反映出的不是臉孔，而是靈魂。

「這真是荒唐！」貓女士不肯靠近池水，但是對池水頗有微詞。忠誠的狗先生無所畏懼，不害怕暴露靈魂，照樣到池邊去喝水。因為在這個世界上，他的心裡只有友愛、善良和奉獻，所以他的靈魂是不會改變的。

而在池水這面神奇的鏡子面前，吉爾俯下身來，幾乎每次都看見一隻光彩奪目的青鳥，因為尋找青鳥的念頭一直佔據他的內心。他懇求光仙子：「請告訴我在哪兒能找到青鳥！妳一定知道！請告訴我吧！」

光仙子神秘莫測地說：「我不能告訴你。你只能靠自己去尋找。」接著光仙子吻了吻吉爾說：「不要灰心！每一次考驗都讓你更加接近青鳥！」

有一天，光仙子對吉爾說：「仙女蓓麗呂捎話來，說一位死者好像把青鳥藏在他的墳墓裡了。青鳥有可能在墓地裡。」

「那怎麼辦呢？」吉爾問。

「很簡單。午夜時，你扭動帽子上的鑽石，死人就會從墓地裡出來的。」

牛奶小姐、水姑娘和糖先生聽了這些話大驚失色，牙齒「喀喀」地抖個不停。

光仙子小聲說：「他們害怕死人，不要理睬他們！」

「我可不怕！」火先生跳躍著說，「從前我常焚燒死人，比現在好玩多了！」

「哦，我覺得快要嘔吐了。」牛奶小姐受不了這種驚嚇。

「我可不怕死人！」狗先生全身哆嗦「不過如果你逃跑，我也跟著逃，而且會非常高興！」

貓女士捋著觸鬚，擺出一貫神秘的語氣說：「我知道其中的秘密！」

「安靜」光仙子說：「仙女有嚴格的命令，只讓吉爾和梅蒂兩個人去，你們和我全都留在墓地門口。」

吉爾非常高興，什麼也沒多想。「妳不和我們一起去嗎？」

他問光仙子。

「不，時機還沒到。」光仙子說：「現在光仙子還不能到死人那裡去。但我不會走遠，你們不必擔心。」

光仙子的話還沒說完，孩子們身邊的一切都變了。神奇的聖堂、閃亮的花朵、美麗的花園眨眼間都不見了，眼前呈現的是一片荒涼的墓地。在柔弱的月光下，有幾座雜草叢生的墳墓立在離他們沒多遠的地方，上面豎著白十字架，一旁是墓碑。吉爾和梅蒂緊緊抱在一起，驚恐極了。

「我好害怕！」梅蒂哭著。

「我向來什麼也不怕。」吉爾說話時結結巴巴。雖然嚇得渾身發抖，但是他不願意承認。

「死人很可怕嗎？」梅蒂問。

「不。」吉爾說：「他們又不是活人！」

「等會兒我們會看見死人嗎？」

吉爾雖然毛骨悚然，但他還是極力裝出若無其事的樣子，但總是不大自然。

「當然，光仙子說能看見。」

「他們在哪兒？」梅蒂問。

吉爾戰戰兢兢地四下環顧著。只有他們兩個人站在墓地裡，一動也不敢動。

「死人在這底下，在這些青草或者大石下面。」

「那是死人的房間門吧？」梅蒂指了指墓碑。

「沒錯。」

「他們天晴時出來嗎？」

「在晚上他們才出來。」

「他們的家很舒適嗎？」

「很狹窄。」

「他們有孩子嗎？」

「那些死了的就是他們的孩子呀！」

「他們靠吃什麼維生呢？」

吉爾想了想，他想死人在地底下不太可能吃地上的東西，於是他肯定地說：「他們吃植物的根！」

梅蒂似乎很滿意這個回答，然後又問起了那個一直困擾著她的問題：「我們能看見他們嗎？」

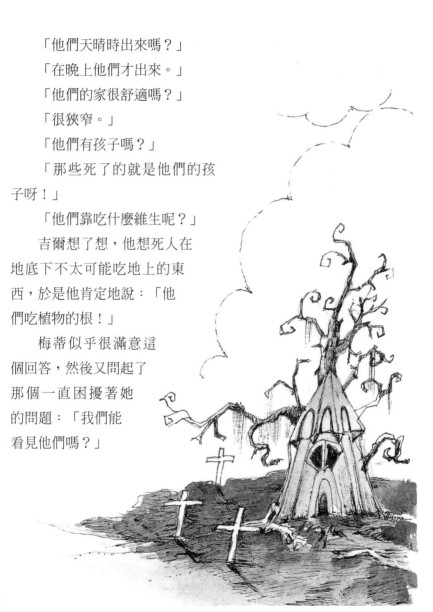

「當然可以。」吉爾說：「只要我轉一下帽子上的鑽石，什麼都能看到。」

這時風吹得樹葉沙沙作響，他們開始感到害怕和孤獨，於是又緊緊地抱在一起說話，這樣才可以打破這可怕的寂靜。

「什麼時候才轉動鑽石？」梅蒂問。

「光仙子說，要到午夜之後才能轉動鑽石，因為午夜時他們會出來呼吸新鮮的空氣，對他們的驚擾會小一些。」

「還沒到午夜嗎？」

吉爾轉身看了看教堂的鐘，時針正好指向十二點。這一下他簡直連說話的力氣都沒了！

吉爾顫抖著說：「聽！快聽！開始要敲鐘了！……聽到了嗎？」

果然時鐘敲了起來。

梅蒂嚇得兩眼發直，跺著腳尖叫道：「快離開這裡！我想離開這裡！」

吉爾也嚇得魂飛魄散，但還算鎮靜一些。「不能離開！我馬上就要轉動鑽石！」

梅蒂哭著說：「不！不！不！我怕！我害怕極了，哥哥，別轉！我想離開這裡！」

吉爾想動手扭動帽上的鑽石，梅蒂卻使勁地抱住他的胳膊，讓他無法伸手摳到鑽石。梅蒂沒命地尖叫著：「我害怕！我不想看見死人！他們一定很可怕！我害怕看到他們！」

時鐘已敲到了第十一下。

「快要錯過了！」吉爾大叫：「就是現在！」

接著他使力掙脫梅蒂，轉動鑽石。

隨著一陣可怕的寂靜，他們看見墳墓裂開了，十字架在搖晃，墓上的石板在慢慢開啓。

梅蒂把臉埋在哥哥的懷中。

「死人出來啦！在那裡！他們在那裡！」梅蒂哭著。

吉爾閉著眼睛，若不是靠著一棵大樹，他早就昏過去了。他不敢動也不敢呼吸，短暫的幾秒鐘彷彿一個世紀那樣漫長。眞奇怪，居然有鳥叫聲！一陣溫馨芬芳的微風拂過他的面頰，溫暖的陽光照在他的手上、脖子上。他疑惑不解，怎麼也想不到會有這樣的奇蹟，他睜開眼睛一看，高興得喊了起來。

原本裂開的墳墓裡開出了成千上萬朵鮮花，花兒到處蔓延著，開在路上、樹梢上、草地上，甚至往上攀爬，像是要戳穿天似的。盛開的花朵全是玫瑰，現出美好金黃的花蕊，放射出明亮的光芒，給孩子們帶來了夏日的溫暖。鳥兒在玫瑰花的周圍歌唱著，蜜蜂也在嗡嗡地歡呼！

「怎麼會是這樣呢？」吉爾說：「怎麼看不到那些墳墓和十字架了？」

兄妹倆迷惑不解，遍地鮮花讓他們眼花繚亂，他們倆牽著手走在「墓地」裡。其實墓地已經消失了，四周只有一座奇妙的花園。他們原本以爲嚇人的骷髏會從墳墓裡爬出來四下裡追趕他們。他們還想像出許許多多可能遇上的可怕情景。現在，展現在他們面前的是世間的眞理。生命永遠存在，它時時變換著新的形

式在不斷延續。當玫瑰謝了，它獻出花粉，孕育出新的一代，它的花瓣還釋放出芬芳的香味；雖然果樹的花都會飄落，但還會長出果實；美麗的蝴蝶還是醜陋的毛毛蟲變的呢。

美麗的鳥兒圍繞吉爾和梅蒂飛著，其中並沒有青鳥，但兩個孩子完全沈浸在自己偉大的發現之中，已經別無所求，只是又驚又喜地喊著：「世界上不存在死亡！世界上不存在死亡！」

一回到光仙子的聖堂，吉爾和梅蒂就舒舒服服地倒在床上。光仙子不想影響他們睡覺，於是吻了吻他們就馬上離開了。

第 8 章
樹林

　　午夜時分，正夢到青衣小孩的吉爾，突然覺得有隻毛茸茸的爪子在自己的臉上撥弄。吉爾被驚醒，坐了起來。在黑暗中有雙眼睛閃閃發亮，吉爾看清是貓女士時，才安下心來。

　　「噓！」貓女士在他耳邊悄悄地說：「不要把他們驚醒。今晚我們只要神不知鬼不覺地溜出去，就一定能抓到青鳥。」

　　吉爾親了親貓女士說：「可是，我們應該向光仙子請示一下，她會很樂意幫助我們的。何況要是瞞著光仙子擅自行動，我會感到不安的。」

　　「如果你告訴了她」貓女士尖聲說道：「那麼一切就都完了，相信我吧，照我的話去做，我們一定能夠成功。」

　　狡猾的貓女士口若懸河地解釋，說吉爾之所以找不到青鳥，全是光仙子的錯，因為他走到哪裡就亮到哪裡。如果現在趁著夜色去找，他們很快就能捉到使人類幸福的青鳥。在貓女士花言巧語的勸說下，吉爾終於被說服了。

　　吉爾、梅蒂和貓女士在皎潔的月光下出發了。

　　「這次我們一定能抓到青鳥的。我已向古老森林中所有的樹打聽過了，青鳥就棲身在他們之中，所以他們都認識青鳥。而且為了多調動一些力量來，我已經派兔子火速去召集重要的動物來

開會了。」貓女士興奮地說著。

　　一小時後，他們到了黑漆漆的森林邊。這時貓女士感覺到她的死對頭，從遠處急匆匆地向他們跑過來。她氣得渾身都在顫抖，難道他要在緊要的關頭搭救孩子們的性命？

　　她湊在吉爾的耳邊甜蜜地說：「眞是遺憾，是我們可敬的朋友狗先生來了。有他跟著，我們的事情可就不妙了。一定得讓他回去，他跟誰都處不來，就連大樹也不例外！」

　　「快回去！現在並不需要你，討厭的傢伙！」吉爾一邊對著狗先生揮揮拳頭，一邊大聲命令著。

聽了吉爾這無情無義的話，蒂魯非常傷心。要是在從前，蒂魯十分聽話，肯定會走開的。但是現在他站在那裡一動也不動，他意識到主人眼下的處境是非常危險的。

　　「難道您就姑息他這種不服從命令的態度嗎？」貓悄聲地對吉爾說：「用棍子打他！」

　　「不要打他！不要這樣！讓蒂魯和我們一起去吧。」梅蒂央求說：「沒有蒂魯在，我會害怕。」

　　他們必須在短時間內做出決定。

　　「我得另外想個法子擺脫這傢伙！」貓女士心裡想著，卻轉身彬彬有禮地對蒂魯說：「真是高興，你能和我們一起去。」

　　於是吉爾和梅蒂並肩緊靠著走向了樹林，貓和狗跟隨在左右兩側。森林裡漆黑一片，他們倆心裡一陣恐懼。這時貓女士大聲叫道：「我們到了！轉動鑽石吧！」

　　吉爾立刻轉動了鑽石！一瞬間四周被照得通明，呈現出奇異的情景。他們正好站在森林的中心，參天大樹都高入雲霄。四下一片死寂，突然間樹葉怪異地抖了起來，樹枝也像人的手臂似地伸展著，樹根從地下崛起，聚攏成腳的形狀。空中一陣陣巨響，樹幹紛紛開裂，每一棵樹中都出現了一個小丑似的樹魂來。

　　貓女士一一將樹魂介紹給他：這是大腹便便的榆樹，他個子矮小，經常牢騷滿腹；山毛櫸樹舉止文雅，風度翩翩；樺樹一身素服，很像吉爾在夜宮中見過的鬼魂；冷杉的個子最高，吉爾無法看到冷杉又高又瘦的軀體上的面目，但冷杉看起來很和藹，帶著一些憂鬱；而冷杉身邊的柏樹一身黑裝，樣子很嚇人。

青鳥

這些樹魂非常高興能夠開口講話，聚在一起沒完沒了地聊著。正當吉爾打算向他們打聽青鳥藏在哪裡時，大夥兒突然都默不作聲。眾多的樹魂紛紛鞠躬施禮，為一棵穿著長袍的千年老橡樹讓出一條路來。老橡樹的長袍上繡滿了苔蘚和地衣，他的白鬍子不時地隨風飄動著。老橡樹已經失明了，他一隻手拄著拐杖，另一隻手扶著一棵為他領路的年輕的橡樹。

「林中之王！」看到老橡樹頭上戴著檞寄生枝做的王冠，吉爾自言自語起來：「我要向他打聽一下青鳥的消息。」

吉爾正要走過去，卻突然驚喜地停住腳步：青鳥就在他的面前，在那棵老橡樹肩上停著呢！

吉爾立刻興奮地叫起來：「青鳥在那裡！快！快！請把牠給我！」

「安靜！不得喧嘩！」眾樹魂驚恐萬分，連忙來喝止吉爾。

「吉爾，請脫帽致意」在一旁的貓女士說：「這位是橡樹大人！」

吉爾馬上照辦。但他萬萬沒想到大難臨頭了，當老橡樹問他是不是樵夫棣爾的兒子時，他毫不猶豫地承認了。

老橡樹立刻氣得渾身發抖，開始指控棣爾犯過的一大堆罪狀：「光是在我們家，你爸爸就殺害了我的六百個兒子、四千七百五十個叔叔嬸嬸、兩千多個兄弟和表姐妹、三百八十個兒媳婦；一萬兩千個曾孫子！」

「找青鳥是為了送給仙女蓓麗呂的小女兒的，她病得很厲害！」吉爾繼續說。

「夠了！」老橡樹打斷了他，「讓我們聽聽動物們的意見！他們在哪兒？我們樹木從來都不獨斷專行。這件事還關係到動物，我們必需一起處理這重大的事件。」

「動物們來了！」冷杉個子比別的樹高，從大大小小的樹頂上望過去，看到了遠處的情況。兔子領頭，後面是馬、母牛、公牛、狼、綿羊、山羊、豬、毛驢，還有熊！

所有的動物都到了。他們用後腿直立行走，穿著人的衣服，一個個神情莊重地在樹中間圍成了一圈。只有舉止輕浮的山羊在路上蹦蹦跳跳，還有不安分的豬，在樹根附近走來走去，想尋找剛剛出土的蘑菇來充饑。

「都到齊了嗎？」老橡樹問。

吉爾小聲對梅蒂說：「真像是富人家的孩子聖誕節時放在聖誕樹上的玩具！多滑稽啊！」

「你們看到的這個孩子」老橡樹大聲說：「從大地母親那裡偷來了法寶，倚仗著寶物想要奪走我們的青鳥，竊取我們那個開天闢地以來一直保持到今天的秘密。我們太瞭解人類了。因此，我們很清楚他得到這個秘密後會如何來對待我們，任何優柔寡斷都是愚蠢的。在這個危急時刻，我們必須馬上將這個孩子除掉，否則就來不及了。」

「他說些什麼？」吉爾問。他還沒有搞清楚老橡樹究竟要幹什麼。

狗先生在老橡樹周圍警惕地徘徊，狗齜著牙齒，低聲咕噥著：「這個老不死的，沒有看見我的牙齒嗎？」

「他竟敢侮辱橡樹大人！」山毛櫸憤怒地說。

「把他趕走！他是叛徒！」老橡樹十分生氣。

「我早就跟你說過吧。」貓女士小聲對吉爾說：「這兒的事情我會安排好的，不過得把蒂魯打發走。」

吉爾對蒂魯說：「快走開！」

「請允許我把這個老東西的苔蘚拖鞋撕破！」蒂魯懇求說。

無論吉爾怎麼勸阻，蒂魯就是不聽。他已意識到主人眼前的危險，更加怒不可遏。貓女士向常春藤求援，蒂魯像瘋了似地衝來衝去，咆哮如雷，並衝著常春藤罵道：「你這團彎彎曲曲的老混球！來呀，你敢？」

周圍的觀眾開始起哄。老橡樹見有人敢藐視自己的權威，氣得臉都白了。但是吉爾疾言厲色，使蒂魯只好乖乖地趴在吉爾腳下。吉爾和梅蒂這時變得束手無策。蒂魯被常春藤又纏又繞，捆得結結實實，然後被綁在栗樹身後最粗的樹根上。

「很好！」老橡樹大著嗓門喊著：「現在我們可以平心靜氣地辦事了。人類對我們的侵害罄竹難書，這是我們第一次有機會來審判人類！因此我想，今天應該怎樣判決他們，大家是不會有什麼異議的。」

樹木和動物們異口同聲地喊道：「死刑！死刑！死刑！」

最初兩個孩子還沒搞清楚。「他們怎麼了，好像不大高興？」吉爾問。

「沒什麼，由於春天姍姍來遲，他們有些生氣了。」貓女士說。然後她又湊近吉爾的耳朵不停地說著，以便分散他的注意。

青鳥

　　就在孩子聽著她的花言巧語時，樹木和動物們正在商量用什麼樣的刑罰來處死這兩個孩子。野牛主張用角抵他們撞死；山毛櫸建議把他們吊死在他最高的樹枝上；常春藤已經準備好了絞刑用的活結；冷杉答應出四塊木板來做棺材；柏樹同意讓出一塊墓碑。

　　柳樹在一旁小聲嘀咕著：「我看最好是把他們扔到河中淹死。」

　　豬哼哼著說：「我看最好把那小女孩吃掉，她的肉應該很嫩！」

　　「住口！」老橡樹吼了起來：「現在我們要決定的，是誰先下手處死他們！」

　　冷杉說：「當然是您有資格！您是我們的國王。」

　　「我太老了！眼瞎體弱，無法擔此重任。」老橡樹說：「這個榮譽應屬於你，就由你來動手替我們討回公道吧！」

　　但是冷杉婉言謝絕了這份光榮，他建議讓質地堅硬的山毛櫸來處理。

　　山毛櫸立刻反對說：「這不行！大家都知道，我的體內生了蛀蟲啦！不如讓榆樹和柏樹來完成這個任務吧。」

　　榆樹一聽立刻叫苦不已，說什麼昨天夜裡鼴鼠咬傷了他的大腳趾，痛得他幾乎站不起來。柏樹也宣稱有病，渾身哆嗦正在發高燒。

　　老橡樹見他們相互推諉，不由得龍顏大怒：「你們這些膽小的傢伙！連這兩個無力抵抗、手無寸鐵的小孩，也把你們嚇成這樣！好吧，我自己來！他們在哪兒？」

老橡樹手拄拐杖，一邊咒罵著，一邊摸索著走向吉爾。

這情景把吉爾給嚇壞了。貓女士突然不見了，說是要想辦法從中調停一下便馬上離去了，再也沒見到她的影子。梅蒂躲在吉爾的懷裡，不停地哆嗦。看著老橡樹氣勢洶洶地逼近他，吉爾覺得孤立無援，但還是像個男子漢那樣抽出隨身帶的小刀迎了上去。

「你這個老不死的，拿著大棍子，是不是來對付我的？」吉爾喊道。

樹木們看到吉爾手中的刀，全嚇得戰戰兢兢，因爲刀是人類所向無敵的武器。他們趕去拉住老橡樹，勸阻他不要動手。老橡樹終因上了年紀，體力不支，扔下了手中的拐杖。

「眞是丟人啊！還是讓動物們來幫我們吧！」老橡樹長歎著說。

梅蒂嚇得尖叫著。

「別怕，我有刀呢！」吉爾極力保護著妹妹。

大公雞叫著：「這個傢伙打算拚命呢！」

「那一個得讓我先吃！」豬貪婪地看著梅蒂。

「我並沒有得罪你們呀！」吉爾說。

「沒得罪，小傢伙。」綿羊說：「只是吃掉了我的一個弟弟、兩個姐姐、三個叔叔、一個姑姑，還有爺爺奶奶。等著吧，當你束手就擒之後，你會知道我也長著牙齒！」

陰險的狼和熊卻不等大家說完，就從背後下手了，他們一下

子把吉爾撲倒在地。其他動物們看到吉爾倒在地上，全都撲了上來。形勢非常危急。吉爾跪著一條腿，揮舞著小刀，梅蒂死命地喊叫。更糟的是，四周突然黑了下來。

吉爾也大聲呼救。「救命啊！蒂魯！蒂魯！……快來救我們！……救命！蒂勒脫快來呀，你在哪兒？」

狡猾的貓女士躲了起來，故意不讓吉爾看見。她假裝嗚咽地說：「我負傷了走不動啦！」

吉爾一邊呼救，一邊竭盡全力護衛著自己，但是寡不敵眾，根本對付不了這麼多動物。他感到性命難保，於是顫抖著再次呼救：「蒂魯！救命！……蒂魯！他們為數眾多，我撐不下去了！」

蒂魯拖著掙脫後拖著繩索「蹭」地躥過來。他狂叫著拍開樹木和動物，跳過去用身體保護他的小主人。

「別怕，小主人！看我怎樣跟他們鬥，怎樣去咬他們！」

吉爾拚命地反抗，他受了傷。

「蒂魯！我們撐不住了，我被榆樹打中了！手在流血！我撐不住了！」吉爾倒在了地上。

蒂魯叫了起來：「有救星了！我們得救了！我聽到他們的腳步聲了！是光仙子！得救了，得救了！看哪！他們害怕啦，他們撤了！小主人，我們得救了！」

果然，光仙子朝他們走來，眼前是一片光明普照，森林裡明亮得如同白晝。

「怎麼回事？發生了什麼意外？」光仙子看到吉爾和梅蒂十分狼狽，蒂魯也遍體鱗傷，大吃一驚：「可憐的孩子，為什麼不趕緊旋轉鑽石呢！」

　　吉爾趕忙照辦。瞬間樹魂都逃回了樹幹，樹幹隨即合上了；動物們的靈魂全消失了，只剩一頭母牛和一隻綿羊在遠處溫馴地吃草，森林恢復了寧靜。吉爾茫然地環視四周。

　　「沒事兒！」吉爾說：「多虧蒂魯，還有我的這把刀。」

　　看到吉爾吃了這麼多的苦頭，光仙子也沒有責備他，更何況剛才他們倆幾乎喪失了生命，使她十分心疼。

　　孩子們和蒂魯都安然無恙，大家高興極了。他們瘋狂地相互親吻；他們一邊歡笑，一邊檢視著身上並不嚴重的傷口。只有貓女士大驚小怪地誇張著說：「我的腳被蒂魯咬傷了！」

　　蒂魯真恨不得咬她一口！他說：「算了，我會一直記得的！」

　　梅蒂責備蒂魯：「別惹她，好嗎？你這個醜八怪！」

　　吉爾非常後悔這次瞞著光仙子擅自行動，因此關於在森林中看見青鳥的事，他連提都不願提起。光仙子卻和藹地對他們倆說：「孩子們！要記住這次教訓！人類本身敵對著世界上的一切！千萬不要忘記。」

第 9 章

道別

　　自從孩子們踏上尋找青鳥的旅途以來，已經過了好多日子，大家道別的時刻馬上就到了。

　　道別的那一天，動物和靜物們都相聚在光仙子聖堂的花園中。光仙子站在大理石陽臺上，望著他們，兄妹倆仍在她身邊沈睡。麵包先生由於太貪吃，現在胖得都無法走路了，靠著善心的牛奶小姐用輪椅推著他；火先生脾氣不好，和所有的人都吵遍了，現在整天悶悶不樂，誰也不搭理他；水姑娘缺少主見，終於答應了糖先生的甜言蜜語，他們倆結婚了；糖先生婚後的模樣極為可憐，都瘦成一把骨頭了，但依然逐日消瘦，而且，一天比一天迷糊，而水姑娘則不再像往日那樣純真自然；貓女士照舊謊話連篇；忠誠的狗先生蒂魯對貓女士還是恨之入骨。

　　光仙子歎了一口氣，心想：「真是可悲！雖然他們獲得了生命，卻沒什麼長進！不是縱欲就是吵架，實在是不可理喻。只有在快要失去幸福時，才能意識到這次機會的重要意義。」

　　這時一隻銀翅膀的鴿子落到了她的膝上，牠的脖上掛著一串翡翠項鍊，繫著一封信，這是仙女蓓麗呂的信差。打開信，光仙子見上面寫著：「切記，時辰已到。」

　　光仙子站起身揮動了手中的魔杖，眼前的一切全都消失了。

幾秒鐘之後，所有的動物、靜物都聚集在一道有小門的高牆外邊。朝陽把樹梢染成一片金色。吉爾和梅蒂醒了。光仙子慈愛地將他們扶起來，他們揉著眼睛，四下環顧，不禁大吃一驚。

光仙子對吉爾說：「怎麼啦？這堵牆，那個小門，難道你們不記得了嗎？」

吉爾搖了搖頭，睡眼惺忪，他一點也想不起了。

光仙子幫助他回憶：「這堵牆圍繞著一棟房子，就是一年前的今天，我們離開了那棟房子……。」

「正好是一年前？這麼說……」吉爾突然向門口跑去，高興地拍起手來：「媽媽一定在裡面！我真想馬上就親親她！馬上！馬上！」

光仙子阻止他說：「現在還太早，你的爸爸和媽媽正睡得香呢，你不應該驚醒他們，何況，時辰未到門是不會開的。」

吉爾問：「什麼時辰？」

「離別的時間。」光仙子有點憂傷地說。

「什麼？您要離開我們嗎？」吉爾急著問。

「我不得不離去了」光仙子說：「沒辦法，時間到了，仙女就要來向你索取青鳥了。」

吉爾著急地叫著：「可我還沒找到青鳥呀！懷念國裡得到的鳥兒變成了黑的；未來王國裡得到的那隻鳥兒飛了；在夜宮裡抓的都死了；墓地裡的那些鳥兒又不是青色的；森林中的那隻我沒抓到！仙女她會怎麼說呢，她會不會生氣？」

「別擔心，孩子。你已盡了最大的努力了。」光仙子說：

「雖然沒有找到青鳥，但是你表現出了膽識、勇氣及善良的心地，你能夠找到青鳥。」

光仙子臉上露出了幸福的微笑。她轉過身，看著哭泣的動物和靜物，叫他們過來與兄妹倆吻別。

「時辰就要到了。大家快向吉爾和梅蒂告別！」光仙子說。

火先生衝上前去，抱住孩子們用力地親吻，吉爾和梅蒂痛得尖叫：「喔！燙死我了！」

「喔！快把我的鼻子燒焦了！」

水姑娘溫柔地走向孩子們說：「別擔心，讓我吻一下就會好的！」

火先生乘機挑撥說：「當心呀！她會把你們淋濕的！」

水姑娘說：「我又溫柔又體貼。我一向是善待人類的。」

「哼！妳又如何解釋淹死那麼多人呢？」對於火先生的責問，水姑娘裝作沒聽見。

「清澈見底的井、淙淙的溪流」水姑娘直接對吉爾和梅蒂說：「不管在哪裡，你們都會找到我。傍晚時坐在泉邊，別忘了傾聽泉水說的話……」

說到這裡，一股淚水從她眼中湧了出來，像瀑布一樣，弄得她渾身都是水，水姑娘不得不停了一下，隨後她又說：「看到水瓶子時，別忘了我！蓄水池裡、水罐裡、在水壺和水龍頭裡，你們都能發現我！」

糖先生一瘸一拐地走了過來，他快站不住了。他用很不自然的聲音說了幾句傷感的話，隨即停住。據他說眼淚和他的個性不

太搭配。

麵包先生喊道：「薄荷糖！」

「糖李子！棒棒糖！焦糖！」火先生怪聲怪氣地叫著。

靜物們都大笑著。吉爾和梅蒂沒有笑容，他們想到就要與靜物們道別，有些傷心。

吉爾問：「蒂魯和蒂勒脫跑到哪裡去了？」

這時，貓女士狼狽地跑過來。她衣服被撕破，毛髮凌亂，臉上摀著一塊手絹，好像牙痛似地呻吟著。狗先生在她身後緊追不捨，連咬帶踢，撲來打去，弄得貓女士十分狼狽。

「知道厲害了吧？」狗先生說：「嘗到了吧！等著瞧吧，後頭還有更厲害的呢！」

光仙子讓狗先生和兄妹倆做最後的吻別，但是他的舌頭一下子變得慘白。

「最……最後一次！」狗先生蒂魯悲痛欲絕，語無倫次，一時不知所措：「我……我們要和他們道別了嗎？」

光仙子說：「是的，時辰就要到了，我們都要恢復成原先的狀態。」

狗先生絕望地叫著，他瘋狂地撲到兩個孩子身上，又是擁抱又是親吻。

「不！不，我不願再做啞巴！我能學會讀書、寫字，和你們一起玩骨牌！我會時刻保持整潔，我再也不偷廚房的東西吃了……」他喊道。

他哭著跪在兩個孩子面前哀求著。吉爾眼睛裡滿是淚水，一

句話也說不出來。梅蒂率真地說：「你是唯一還沒和我們吻別的，蒂勒脫！」

貓女士矯柔造作地說：「孩子們，我當然很熱愛你們嘍！」

然後是一陣沈默。

光仙子說話了：「現在，該我和你們吻別了。」

說著，光仙子用她的斗篷把吉爾和梅蒂圍了起來，彷彿這是她最後一次以她的光輝來庇護這兩個孩子。然後她分別給吉爾和梅蒂又久又摯愛的親吻，兩個孩子緊拉著她懇求。

「請不要走，不要走，和我們待在一起吧！」孩子們哭著：「我們會讓媽媽知道妳對我們多麼好，爸爸不會有意見的。」

光仙子對他們說了一些讓人難忘的話，然後如同母親一般示意他們安靜下來。

「吉爾，聽我說，要記住，在世界上你們看見的一切都沒有開始，也沒有結束，永遠在延續。你們應該永遠記得這個道理，讓它隨著你成長。那麼，不管遇到什麼情況，你們都會知道應該期待什麼、說什麼、做些什麼。」

光仙子繼續深情地對哭泣的吉爾和梅蒂說：「我可愛的孩子們，別哭了，我只能發出人們不易理解的光，不能像水姑娘那樣發出聲音。可是我始終在關照著人們的一生。別忘了，我是在用光線和你們說話的：靠著噴薄而出的陽光、普照萬物的月光、閃爍的星光、一盞盞燈光，還有你們的美好善良、積極進取的心靈之光⋯⋯」

那座爺爺留下的鐘敲響了八下，光仙子小聲地說，但聲音越來越微弱:「再見了,時辰到了!……再見!再見!」

　　光仙子的身影越來越模糊。透過淚眼,兄妹倆看到光仙子化成了一道光線,消失在他們的面前,動物和靜物們也都不見了。

第 10 章
甦醒

　　爺爺生前留下的老式大座鐘已經敲響了八下，在樵夫的小屋子裡，吉爾和梅蒂還在床上睡著。媽媽將圍裙撩起掖在腰上、雙手叉腰，站在床邊看著兄妹倆，微笑著責備說：「起床，你們這兩個懶骨頭！可不能讓你們貪睡到中午！」

　　媽媽在吉爾身上輕輕地拍了一下，吉爾把眼睛睜開，嘴裡嘀咕著：「光仙子？你在哪兒？什麼？不！不！你別走開！」

　　媽媽笑著說：「光？當然有啦！光線出來很久了！」

　　「媽媽！是你呀！媽媽！」吉爾揉著眼睛叫道。他好久好久沒見到媽媽了，興奮得快要發瘋，使勁地親吻著媽媽。

　　媽媽心裡有些不安，兒子說走了很遠的路，和他一起去的還有仙女呀、牛奶呀、糖果呀、水呀、火呀、麵包呀、光仙子呀！還說他離家已經整整一年了！

　　媽媽被吉爾嚇了一跳。她大聲說道：「可是你根本就沒離開這個屋子！昨晚我送你上床，今天早上你就在這兒呀！今天是聖誕節，你沒聽見村子裡的鐘聲嗎？」

　　「我是在一年前的聖誕夜出發的，」吉爾固執地說：「你沒生氣吧？是不是很傷心？爸爸怎麼說呢？」

　　吉爾依然滔滔不絕地說著：「呵！太驚險了！不信你去問梅

蒂。我們在懷念國裡見到了爺爺奶奶！真的，懷念國就在我們走過的路上。雖然爺爺奶奶死了，身體卻都很健康。對不對呀，梅蒂？」

梅蒂也醒了，跟著哥哥一起描述他們如何看到了爺爺奶奶，以及死去的兄弟姊妹們，他們有多麼開心。

媽媽跑到門口，用盡全力對著正在森林邊緣工作的丈夫大喊。

「天哪！天哪！親愛的，快回來！快！」她高聲叫著：「我不能再失去吉爾和梅蒂了，我已失去好幾個孩子了！」

爸爸很快就回到屋裡，不等他放下手裡的斧頭，兩個孩子就把他們的奇遇講了出來，然後問爸爸過去年一年都做些什麼。

「你看！你看，他們倆昏頭了！」媽媽哭著說：「要出事了！快去叫醫生來呀！」

但是爸爸一向鎮定自若，他親了親孩子們，安然地點燃煙斗，說孩子們的臉色很好，沒必要著急。

這時候，響起一聲敲門聲，鄰居老奶奶走了進來。老奶奶拄著拐杖，身材矮小，很像仙女蓓麗呂。兄妹倆立刻張開雙臂抱住她，在她身邊雀躍不已，並且喊道：「是仙女蓓麗呂！」

老奶奶向吉爾的媽媽開口說：「聖誕節了，我過來想借點火，燉點菜……今天早上真冷！早晨太冷了。早安，孩子們！」

吉爾這時心裡卻忐忑不安，但他勇敢地走到老奶奶面前說：「仙女蓓麗呂，我沒有找到青鳥。」

「你說什麼？」老奶奶聽了吉爾這句沒頭沒腦的話，嚇了一

跳。「蓓麗……什麼？」

吉爾不慌不忙地回答：「蓓麗呂。」

「柏林考脫，你說的是柏林考脫。」鄰居老奶奶說。

聽老奶奶堅決地否認她是仙女，吉爾有一點不高興地說：「隨您怎麼說，蓓麗呂也好，柏林考脫也好，可是我知道我在說什麼。」

爸爸很不耐煩了。「給他兩個耳光算了，別再讓他沒完沒了地胡說了！」

「別這樣，不值得為了這事打孩子！」老奶奶說：「他倆一定是做了怪夢，一定是在他們沈睡時月光照在臉上了，我那個患重病的小女兒也經常如此。」柏林考脫太太搖了搖頭說：「醫生說是因為她的神經，可我還是不知道什麼能治她的病，早上她還向我要件東西做聖誕禮物。」

她看了看吉爾，猶豫了一下，然後歎著氣無可奈何地說：「她著了迷，一心想要那個東西，我能怎麼辦呢？」

大家知道柏林考脫太太的話是什麼意思，她的小女兒常說，如果吉爾能把鴿子給她，她的病就會好。但吉爾就是捨不得給她那隻自己喜歡的鴿子。

「孩子，那個小姑娘太可憐了。」媽媽問吉爾，「你願不願意把鴿子給她？她一直很渴望得到那隻鴿子！」

「鴿子！」吉爾拍了一下腦袋叫起來，好像他們這事已解決了似的。「我的鴿子！」他在鳥籠底下放了一隻椅子，興高采烈地爬了上去，嘴裡說：「當然，我願意送她！當然願意！」

突然，眼前的情景讓他驚呆了：「咦！這是我的那隻鴿子嗎？怎麼會是青色的？還是原來那隻鴿子，但在我離開的時候變成青的了！」

　　吉爾高興得從椅子上跳下來，一邊跑一邊喊：「這就是我們四處找的那隻青鳥！我們跋山涉水到處找牠，牠卻在這兒！哈！這太奇妙了！牠在家裡啊！梅蒂，看見青鳥了嗎？光仙子知道了會怎麼說？拿去吧，柏林考脫太太，快給妳的小女兒！」

　　柏林考脫太太面帶笑容，合攏雙手不停地道謝。吉爾把鴿子捧給她時，她簡直不相信這是真的。她把吉爾緊緊地抱在懷裡，禁不住流下了眼淚。

　　「送給我了嗎？」她不停地問：「就這樣把牠給我嗎？你真的送給我了？天哪！我女兒會多高興呀！我立刻拿給她，然後看看她會說些什麼。」

　　「好啊，好啊，快去吧！有些鳥兒會變色的！」吉爾催促著。

　　等柏林考脫太太跑出了門，吉爾把門關好。他感到四周的一切都變得十分美好，隨著他對世界的理解更加純真透徹，在他眼中的世界會顯得更加美好。

　　吉爾充滿快樂地觀察著屋裡的一切。他俯下身來，對著麵包鍋裡的麵包客套了一番，又跑到睡在窩裡還沒起床的蒂魯跟前，稱讚蒂魯在森林裡的勇敢出色。

　　梅蒂蹲下來撫摸著正趴在爐火旁打呼嚕的蒂勒脫說：「喂！蒂勒脫！我知道你認識我，但是再也不能聽到你講話了！」

吉爾伸手摸著額頭。他叫了起來：「唉呦！鑽石不見了！誰拿走了我的綠色小帽！算了，拿走了也沒關係，反正我用不著它了。哈！火先生，早安！瞧他又在惹水姑娘生氣了！」他擰開水龍頭，俯下身對水說：「早安，水姑娘！妳說了些什麼？再也聽不懂妳的話了。哈！我多麼幸福！太幸福了！」

　　梅蒂也跟著喊道：「我也很幸福！和你一樣！」。

　　兄妹倆拉著手在廚房裡蹦呀跳呀，開心極了。

　　媽媽看著兩個孩子精神抖擻，生氣勃勃，稍微放心了一點兒。爸爸平靜地坐在那裡笑著吃粥。

　　「瞧」爸爸在一旁說：「他們在想像中玩幸福生活的遊戲呢！」

　　他們不是玩幸福生活的遊戲，而是在夢中學會了體會生活中的幸福，這是最重要、最難學的一課。

　　吉爾對踮著腳站在窗邊的梅蒂說：「看！光仙子，她在那兒！透過樹梢從樹林裡照射下來……」

　　突然吉爾不說話了，側起耳朵，一家人都在聽著，他們聽到了越來越近的歡笑聲。

　　吉爾叫道：「是光仙子！我去開門！」

　　其實是鄰居柏林考脫和她的小女兒。

　　柏林考脫太太興奮地而：「看呀！真是奇怪！現在她能跑、能跳，幾乎能飛了！她一看到這隻鴿子，就這樣跳了起來！」

　　說著，柏林考脫太太竟兩腿交替著跳了起來，也不怕摔扁她的彎鼻子。

大家全都大笑起來，孩子們不停地拍著手。

小女孩站在廚房中間，穿著白色的長睡衣。病了這麼久，竟然能自己走動了。她微笑著把吉爾的鴿子緊緊地抱在胸前，現在居然站起來了。

吉爾望著小女孩，又望著梅蒂說：「她多像光仙子啊！」

「就是個子矮了點。」梅蒂說。

「嗯，有點兒矮。」吉爾說：「不過她會長高呀！」

三個孩子都拿了一點吃的餵鴿子。大人們放心了，微笑地看著他們。

吉爾滿臉笑容，沈浸在幸福中。鴿子的顏色其實並沒變，是吉爾的心中充滿了快樂和幸福，使鴿子在他的眼中光彩奪目，呈現出青色。吉爾不知不覺地發現了光仙子最最重要的秘密，那就是：給他人幸福，自己才更接近幸福。

這時大家慌亂了起來，孩子們尖叫著，大人們伸出雙臂向門口衝去。鴿子突然飛跑啦！牠迅速地飛著！越飛越遠。

小女孩啜泣著：「鴿子！我的鴿子！」

吉爾第一個爬上梯子，然後又興沖沖地跑回來。

「別哭！沒有關係，牠還在屋裡！」吉爾說：「會找到牠的。」

吉爾吻了吻小姑娘，小姑娘終於破涕為笑。

「你一定能再找到牠嗎？」小姑娘問。

吉爾充滿信心地說：「相信我，我知道哪裡能找到！」

親愛的讀者，現在你們也明白青鳥會在什麼地方了吧。

1

THE WOODCUTTER'S COTTAGE

It was Christmas Eve, Mummy put her little ones to bed and kissed them even more lovingly than usual. Mummy felt a little sad because, owing to the stormy weather, Daddy Tyl was not able to go to work in the forest; and so she had no money to buy presents with which to fill Tyltyl and Mytyl's stockings. The Children soon fell asleep, everything was still and silent and not a sound was heard but the purring of the cat, the snoring of the dog and the ticking of the clock. But suddenly a light as bright as day crept through the shutters, the lamp upon the table lit again of itself and the two Children awoke, yawned, rubbed their eyes, stretched out their arms in bed and Tyltyl, in a cautious voice called:

"Mytyl?"

"Yes, Tyltyl?" was the answer.

"Are you asleep?"

"Are you?"

"No," said Tyltyl. "How can I be asleep, when I'm talking to you?"

"I say, is this Christmas Day?" asked his sister.

"Not yet; not till tomorrow. But Santa Claus won't bring us anything this year."

"Why not?"

"I heard Mummy say that she couldn't go to town to ask him to come. But he will come next year."

"Is next year far off?"

"A good long while," said the boy with a sigh. "But he will come to the rich children tonight."

"Really?"

"Look!" cried Tyltyl of a sudden. "Mummy has forgotten to put out the lamp! Let's get up."

"But we mustn't." said Mytyl, who always remembered what mummy told her.

"Why, there's no one around! Do you see the shutters?"

"Oh, how bright they are!"

"It's the lights of the party," said Tyltyl.

"What party?"

"The rich children opposite. It's the Christmas tree. Let's open the shutters."

Mytyl asked timidly: "Can we?"

"Of course we can; there's no one to stop us··· Do you hear the music? ··· Let us get up."

The two Children jumped out of the bed, ran to the window, climbed on the stool in front of it and threw back the shutters. A bright light filled the room; and the Children looked out eagerly.

"We can see everything!" said Tyltyl.

"I can't." said poor little Mytyl, who could hardly find room on the stool.

"It's snowing!" said Tyltyl. "There are two carriages, with six horses each!"

"There are twelve little boys getting out!" said Mytyl, who was

doing her best to peep out of the window.

"Don't be silly! They're little girls."

"But they've got knickerbockers on…"

"Do be quiet! And Look! It's Christmas tree."

"What are those gold things there, hanging from the branches?"

"Why, toys, to be sure!" said Tyltyl. "Swords, guns, soldiers, cannons…"

"And what's that, all round the table?"

"Cakes and fruit and cream tarts."

"Oh, how pretty the children are!" cried Mytyl, clapping her hands.

"And how they're laughing and laughing!" answered Tyltyl.

"And the little ones dancing!"

"Yes, yes. Let's dance too!" shouted Tyltyl.

And the two Children began to stamp their feet for joy on the stool.

"Oh, what fun!" said Mytyl.

"They're getting the cakes!" cried Tyltyl. "They can touch them… They're eating, they're eating, they're eating! Oh… How lovely, how lovely!"

Mytyl began to count imaginary cakes. "I have twelve!"

"And I four times twelve!" said Tyltyl. "But I'll give you some…"

And our little friends, dancing, laughing and shrieking with delight, rejoiced so prettily in the other children's happiness that they forgot their own poverty and want. Suddenly, there came a loud knocking at the door. The startled Children ceased their romp and

dared not move a limb. Then the big wooden latch lifted of itself, with a loud creak; the door opened slowly; and in crept a little old woman, dressed all in green, with a red hood over her head. She was hump-backed and lame and had only one eye; her nose and chin almost touched; and she walked leaning on a stick. She was surely a fairy.

She hobbled up to the Children and asked, in a snuffling voice:

"Have you the bird that is blue?"

"Tyltyl has a bird," said Mytyl.

"But I can't give it away, because it's mine," the little fellow added, quickly.

The Fairy put on her big, round glasses and looked at the bird. "He's not blue enough," she exclaimed: "I must absolutely have the Blue Bird. It's for my little girl, who is very ill···" The Fairy raised her crooked finger to her long, pointed nose, and whispered, in a mysterious tone. "The Blue Bird stands for happiness; and I want you to understand that my little girl must be happy in order to get well. That is why I now command you to go out into the world and find the Blue Bird for her. You will have to start at once··· Do you know who I am?"

The Children exchanged puzzled glances and Tyltyl soon said politely: "You are rather like our neighbor, Madame Berlingot···"

Goody Berlingot had a dear little girl who used to play on Sundays with the woodcutter's Children. Unfortunately, the poor little pretty, fair-haired thing was always suffering from some unknown complaint, which often kept her in bed. When this happened, she used to beg and pray for Tyltyl's dove to play with; but Tyltyl was so fond of the bird that he would not give it to her. All this, thought the little boy, was very like that which the Fairy told him; and that was why he

called her Berlingot.

Much to his surprise, the Fairy turned crimson with rage. "What do I look like?" she asked Tyltyl. "Am I pretty or ugly? Old or young?"

Her reason for asking these questions was to try the kindness of the little boy. He turned away his head and dared not say what he thought of her looks. Then she cried: "I am the Fairy Bérylune!"

As the Children were still in their nightshirts, the Fairy told them to get dressed. She herself helped Mytyl and, while she did so, asked: "Where are your Father and Mother?"

"In there," said Tyltyl, pointing to the door on the right. "They're asleep."

"And your Grandad and Granny?"

"They're dead.

"And your little brothers and sisters··· Have you any?"

"Oh, yes, three little brothers!" said Tyltyl.

"And four little sisters," added Mytyl.

"Where are they?" asked the Fairy.

"They are dead, too," answered Tyltyl.

"Would you like to see them again?"

"Oh, yes! At once! Show them to us!"

"I haven't them in my pocket," said the Fairy. "But this is very lucky; you will see them when you go through the Land of Memory. It's on the way to the Blue Bird, just on the left, past the third turning··· What were you doing when I knocked?"

"We were playing at eating cakes," said Tyltyl.

"Have you any cakes? Where are they?"

"In the house of the rich children··· Come and look, it's so

lovely!"

And Tyltyl dragged the Fairy to the window.

"But it's the others who are eating them!" said she.

"Yes, but we can see them eat," said Tyltyl.

"Aren't you mad at them?"

"What for?"

"For eating all the cakes. I think it's very wrong of them not to give you any."

"Not at all; they're rich··· I say, isn't it beautiful over there?"

"It's just the same here, only you can't see···"

"Yes, I can," said Tyltyl. "I have very good eyes. I can see the time on the church clock; and Daddy can't!"

The Fairy suddenly grew angry and cried out: "I tell you that you can't see!"

And she grew angrier and angrier. As though it mattered about seeing the time on the church clock!

Of course, the little boy was not blind; but, as he was kind-hearted and deserved to be happy, she wanted to teach him to see what is good and beautiful in all things. It was not an easy task, for she well knew that most people live and die without enjoying the happiness that lies all around them. Still, as she was a fairy, she was all-powerful; and so she decided to give him a little hat adorned with a magic diamond that would possess the extraordinary property of always showing him the truth, which would help him to see the inside of Things and thus teach him that each of them has a life and an existence of its own, created to match and gladden ours.

The Fairy took the little hat from a great bag hanging by her side. It was green and had a white cockade, with the big diamond shining in

the middle of it. Tyltyl was beside himself with delight. The Fairy explained to him how the diamond worked. By pressing the top, you saw the soul of Things; if you gave it a little turn to the right, you discovered the Past; and, when you turned it to the left, you beheld the Future.

Tyltyl beamed all over his face and danced for joy; and then he at once became afraid of losing the little hat. "Daddy will take it from me!" he cried.

"No," said the Fairy, "for no one can see it as long as it's on your head··· Will you try it?"

"Yes, yes!" cried the Children, clapping their hands.

The hat was no sooner on the little boy's head than a magic change came over everything. The old Fairy turned into a young and beautiful princess, dressed all in silk and covered with sparkling jewels; the walls of the cottage became transparent and gleamed like precious stones; the humble deal furniture shone like marble. The two children ran from right to left clapping their hands and shouting with delight.

But further and much greater surprises were in store for them. Lo and behold, suddenly the door of the grandfather's clock opened, the silence was filled with the sweetest music and twelve little daintily-dressed and laughing dancers began to skip and spin all around the Children.

"They are the Hours of your life," said the Fairy. Tyltyl gazed with admiration at those pretty creatures, who seemed to skim over the floor like birds.

But just then a funny fat fellow, all out of breath and covered with flour, who came struggling out of the bread-pan and bowing to the children. It was Bread! He had hardly tumbled out of his pan,

when other loaves followed after and began to frisk about with the Hours, without giving a thought to the flour which they scattered over those pretty ladies and which wrapped them in great white clouds.

The Hours waltzed with the loaves; the plates, the glasses, the forks, and the knives joining in the fun, hopped up and down, clinked together that you could not hear for the noise···

When the romp was at its height, an enormous flame darted out of the chimney and filled the room with a great red glow, as though the house were on fire. Everybody bolted into the corners in dismay, While Tyltyl and Mytyl, sobbing with fright, hid their heads under the good Fairy's cloak.

"Don't be afraid," she said. "It's only Fire, who has come to join in your fun. He is a good sort, but you had better not touch him, for he has a hot temper."

The Children saw a tall, red fellow. When he waved his long arms, silk scarves hung from his shoulders were just like flames; and his hair stood up on his head in straight, flaring locks. He started flinging out his arms and legs and jumping round the room like a madman.

Then the Fairy Bérylune pointed her wand at the tap; and at once there appeared a young girl who wept like a regular fountain. It was Water. She was very pretty, had nothing on but her bed-gown; but the water that streamed over her clothed her in shimmering colors. As soon as she caught sight of Fire still whirling around like a great madcap, she made an angry and indignant rush at him, spraying his face, splashing and wetting him with all her might. Fire flew into a rage and began to smoke.

Suddenly, a startling noise of breaking crockery made the Children look round towards the table. What a surprise! The milk-jug lay on the floor, smashed into a thousand fragments, and from the pieces rose a charming lady, who gave little screams of terror and clasped her hands and turned up her eyes with a beseeching glance.

Meanwhile, the sugar-loaf, which also seemed to be coming to life. Packed in its blue paper wrapper, it was swaying from left to right and from right to left. A long thin arm was seen to come out, followed by a peaked head, which split the paper, and by another arm and two long legs that seemed never to end! Oh, you should have seen how funny Sugar looked: so funny, indeed, that the Children could not help laughing in his face!

"Bow, wow, wow! Good morning! Good morning, my little god! At last, at last we can talk! Bark and wag my tail as I might, you never understood! I love you! I love you!"

Tyltyl and Mytyl know him at once. It is Tylo, the good-natured Animal who goes with the Children to the forest, the faithful guardian who protects the door, the staunch friend who is ever true and ever loyal! Here he comes walking on his hind-paws, as on a pair of legs too short for him, and beating the air with the two others, making gestures like a clumsy little man. And it is a pretty sight to see him kissing his little master and mistress and calling them "his little gods!"

But Tylo's heart felt a pang when he saw Tylette, the Cat, coming to life in her turn and being petted and kissed by the Children. Tylo felt bitter in his heart.

In the meantime, the Cat, who had begun by washing herself and polishing her claws, calmly put out her paw to the little girl. She said to Mytyl: "Good morning, miss! How well you look this morning!" And the Children patted her like anything.

At that moment, a great thing had happened. At eleven o' clock in the evening, in the middle of that winter's night, a great light, the light of the noonday sun, glowing and dazzling, burst into the cottage.

At the window, in the center of a great halo of sunshine, there rose slowly, like a tall golden sheaf, a maiden of surpassing loveliness! Gleaming veils covered her figure without hiding its beauty; her bare arms, stretched in the attitude of giving, seemed transparent; and her great clear eyes wrapped all upon whom they fell in a fond embrace.

"It's the Queen!" said Tyltyl.

"No, my Children," said the Fairy. "It is Light!"

Smiling, Light stepped towards the two little ones. She, the Light of Heaven, the strength and beauty of the Earth, was proud of the humble mission entrusted to her. She's here to lead the Children out into the world and teach them to know that other Light, the Light of

the Mind.

"It is Light!" exclaimed the Things and the Animals; and, as they all loved her, they began to dance around her with cries of pleasure. Tyltyl and Mytyl capered with joy. Never had they pictured so amusing and so pretty a party; and they shouted louder than all the rest.

Suddenly, three knocks were heard against the wall, loud enough to throw the house down! It was Daddy Tyl, who had been waked up by the din and who was now threatening to come and put a stop to it.

"Turn the diamond!" cried the Fairy to Tyltyl.

Our hero hastened to obey, but he had not the knack of it yet; besides, his hand shook at the thought that his father was coming. In fact, he was so awkward that he nearly broke the works.

"Not so quick, not so quick!" said the Fairy. "Oh dear, you've turned it too briskly: they will not have time to resume their places and we shall have a lot of bother!"

There was a general stampede. The walls of the cottage lost their splendor. All ran hither and thither, to return to their proper shape: Fire could not find his chimney; Water ran around looking for her tap; Sugar stood moaning in front of his torn wrapper; and Bread, the biggest of the loaves, was unable to squeeze into his pan, in which the other loaves had jumped higgledy-piggledy, taking up all the room. As for the Dog, he had grown too large for the hole in his kennel; and the Cat also could not get into her basket. The Hours alone, who were accustomed always to run faster than Man wished, had slipped back into the clock without delay.

Light stood motionless and unruffled, vainly setting an example of calmness to the others, who were all weeping and wailing around

the Fairy:

"What is going to happen?" they asked. "Is there any danger?"

"Well," said the Fairy, "I am bound to tell you the truth: all those who accompany the two Children will die at the end of the journey."

They began to cry like anything, all except the Dog, who was delighted at remaining human as long as possible and who had already taken his stand next to Light, so as to be sure of going in front of his little master and mistress.

At that moment, there came a knocking even more dreadful than before.

"There's Daddy again!" said Tyltyl. "He's getting up, this time; I can hear him walking···"

"You see," said the Fairy, "you have no choice now; it is too late; you must all start with us··· And you shall all come to my house, where I will dress the Animals and the Things properly··· Let us go out this way!"

As she spoke, she pointed her wand at the window, which lengthened magically downwards, like a door. They all went out on tiptoe, after which the window resumed its usual shape. And so it came about that, on Christmas Night, in the clear light of the moon, while the bells rang out lustily, proclaiming the birth of Jesus, Tyltyl and Mytyl went in search of the Blue Bird that was to bring them happiness.

2

AT THE FAIRY'S

They had hardly reached the highroad, when the Fairy remembered that they could not walk like that through the village, which was still lit up because of the feast. She pressed lightly on Tyltyl's head and willed that they should all be carried by magic to her palace. Then and there, a cloud of fireflies surrounded our companions and wafted them gently towards the sky. They were at the Fairy's palace before they had recovered from their surprise.

"Follow me," she said and led them through chambers and passages all in gold and silver. They stopped in a large room surrounded with mirrors on every side and containing an enormous wardrobe with light creeping through its chinks. The Fairy Bérylune took a diamond key from her pocket and opened the wardrobe.

One cry of amazement burst from every throat. Mantles covered with gems, dresses of every sort and every country, pearl coronets, emerald necklaces, ruby bracelets··· Never had the Children beheld such riches! As for the Things, their state was rather one of utter bewilderment.

Fire, who only cared for red, at once chose a splendid bright red dress, with gold spangles. He put nothing on his head, for his head was always very hot. The long blue and white dress which Sugar selected and the pointed hat, like a candle extinguisher, which he wore on his head made him look perfectly ridiculous. The Cat put on a suit

of black tights, with jet embroidery, hung a long velvet cloak from her shoulders and perched a large cavalier hat, with a long feather, on her neat little head. She next asked for a pair of soft kid boots, in memory of Puss-in-Boots, her distinguished ancestor, and put a pair of gloves on her forepaws, to protect them from the dust of the roads.

Thus attired, she hastily invited Sugar and Fire to take the air with her.

So they all three walked out, while the others went on dressing. After passing through several splendid galleries, they stopped in the hall; and the Cat at once addressed the meeting in a hushed voice: "I have brought you here," she said, "in order to discuss the position in which we are placed. Let us make the most of our last moment of liberty…"

But she was interrupted by a furious uproar: "Bow, wow, wow!"

"There now!" cried the Cat. "There's that idiot of a Dog! He has scented us out! We can't get a minute's peace. Let us hide behind the balustrade. He had better not hear what I have to say to you."

"It's too late," said Sugar, who was standing by the door.

And, sure enough, Tylo was coming up, jumping, barking, panting and delighted.

The Cat, when she saw him, turned away in disgust: "He has put on the livery of one of the footmen of Cinderella's coach… It is just the thing for him: he has the soul of a flunkey!"

She ended

these words with a "Fft! Fft!" and, stroking her whiskers, took up her stand, with a defiant air, between Sugar and Fire. The good Dog danced round and round. It was really funny to see his velvet coat whirling like a merry-go-round, with the skirts opening every now and then and showing his little stumpy tail.

"There!" he said. "There! Aren't we fine! Just look at this lace and embroidery! It's real gold and no mistake!" He did not see that the others were laughing at him. He had also encased his hind-legs, in a pair of patent-leather riding-boots, with white tops; but his forepaws he considered of such use that nothing would have induced him to put them into gloves. Tylo had too natural a character to change his little ways all in a day. He was at the present moment lying on the steps of the hall, scratching the ground and sniffing at the wall.

Suddenly a very sweet song came from the distance. The song drew nearer, a girl's fresh voice filled the shadows of the lofty arches and Water appeared. A beautiful silvery dress waved and floated around her; and her hair decked with corals flowed below her knees.

When Fire caught sight of her, like the rude and spiteful fellow that he was, he sneered: "She's not brought her umbrella!"

But Water, who was really quite witty and who knew that she was the stronger of the two, chaffed him pleasantly and said, with a glance at his glowing nose: "I beg your pardon? I thought you might be speaking of a great red nose I saw the other day!"

The others began to laugh and poke fun at Fire, whose face was always like a red-hot coal.

A shapeless and ridiculous bulk, clad in all the colors of the rainbow, came and blocked the narrow door of the hall. It was the enormous stomach of Bread, who filled the whole opening. He was pleased all the same: "Here I am!" he said. "Here I am! I have put on Bluebeard's finest dress··· What do you think of this?"

The Dog began to frisk around him: he thought Bread magnificent! That yellow velvet, costume, covered all over with silver crescents, reminded Tylo of the delicious horseshoe rolls which he loved; and the huge, gaudy turban on Bread's head was really very like a fairy bun!

"How nice he looks!" he cried. "How nice he looks!"

Bread was shyly followed by Milk. Sher prefer cream dress to all the finery which the Fairy suggested to her.

The Cat cut everyone short in a masterful voice: "Stop chattering, listen to me, time presses: our future is at stake···"

They all looked at her with a bewildered air. The Cat, becoming

impatient, continued her speech: "The Fairy has just said it, the end
of this journey will, at the same time, mark the end of our lives. It is
our business, therefore, to spin the journey out as long as possible and
by every means in our power···"

Bread hastened to express approval; but the Dog pretending not
to hear, began to growl deep down in his soul; and, when Tylette
ended her speech with the words, "We must at all costs prolong the
journey and prevent Blue Bird from being found, even if it means
endangering the lives of the Children," the good Dog, obeying only
the promptings of his heart, leapt at the Cat to bite her. Sugar, Bread
and Fire flung themselves between them: "Order! Order!" said
Bread pompously. "I'm in the chair at this meeting."

"Who made you chairman?" stormed Fire.

"Who asked you to, interfere?" asked Water, whirling her wet
hair over Fire.

"Excuse me," said Sugar, shaking all over, in conciliatory
tones. "Excuse me··· This is a serious moment··· Let us talk things
over in a friendly way."

"I quite agree with Sugar and the Cat," said Bread.

"This is ridiculous!" said the Dog, barking and showing his
teeth. "There is Man and that's all! We have to obey him and do as
he tells us! I recognize no one but him! Hurrah for Man! Man forever!
In life or death, all for Man! Man is everything!"

But the Cat's shrill voice rose above all the others: "All of us
here present," she cried, "Animals, Things and Elements, possess a
soul which Man does not yet know. That is why we retain a remnant
of independence; but, if he finds the Blue Bird, he will know all, he
will see all and we shall be completely at his mercy. Remember the

time when we wandered at liberty upon the face of the earth!" Suddenly her face changed, her voice sank to a whisper and she hissed, "Look out! I hear the Fairy and Light coming. I need hardly tell you that Light has taken sides with Man and means to stand by him; she is our worst enemy⋯ Be careful!"

The Fairy exclaimed the moment she appeared upon the threshold: "What are you doing in that corner? You look like a pack of conspirators!"

Tyltyl and Mytyl stood hand in hand in front of the Fairy, looking a little frightened and a little awkward in their fine clothes.

They stared at each other in childish admiration.

The little girl was wearing a yellow silk frock embroidered with pink posies and covered with gold spangles. On her head was a lovely orange velvet cap; and a starched muslin tucker covered her little arms. Tyltyl was dressed in a red jacket and blue knickerbockers, both of velvet; and of course he wore the wonderful little hat on his head.

The Fairy said to them: "It is just possible that the Blue Bird is hiding at your grandparents' in the Land of Memory; so you will go there first."

"But how shall we see them, if they are dead?" asked Tyltyl.

Then the good Fairy explained that they would not be really dead until their grandchildren ceased to think of them: "Men do not know this secret," she added. "But, thanks to the diamond, you, Tyltyl, will see that the dead whom we remember live as happily as though they were not dead."

"Are you coming with us?" asked the boy, turning to Light, who stood in the doorway and lit up all the hall.

"No," said the Fairy. "Light must not look at the past. Her energies must be devoted to the future!"

The two Children were starting on their way, when they discovered that they were very hungry. The Fairy at once ordered Bread to give them something to eat; and that big, fat fellow, delighted with the importance of his duty, undid the top of his robe, drew his scimitar and cut two slices out of his belly. The Children screamed with laughter. Sugar, who was very full of himself, also wanted to impress the company and, breaking off two of his fingers, handed them to the astonished Children.

As they were all moving towards the door, the Fairy Bérylune

stopped them: "Not today," she said. "The children must go alone. It would be indiscreet to accompany them; they are going to spend the evening with their late family. Come, be off! Good bye, dear children, and mind that you are back in good time: it is extremely important!"

The two Children took each other by the hand and, carrying the big cage, passed out of the hall; and their companions, at a sign from the Fairy, filed in front of her to return to the palace. Our friend Tylo was the only one who did not answer to his name. The moment he heard the Fairy say that the Children were to go alone, he had made up his mind to go and look after them, whatever happened; and, while the others were saying good bye, he hid behind the door. But the poor fellow had reckoned without the all-seeing eyes of the Fairy Bérylune.

"Tylo!" she cried. "Tylo! Here!" And the poor Dog, who had so long been used to obey, dared not resist the command and came, with his tail between his legs, to take his place among the others. He howled with despair when he saw his little master and mistress swallowed up in the great gold staircase.

3

THE LAND OF MEMORY

The Land of Memory was not far off; but to reach it they had to go through a forest that was so dense and so old that their eyes could not see the tops of the trees. It was always shrouded in a heavy mist; and the Children would certainly have lost their way, if the Fairy had not said to them beforehand: "It is straight ahead; and there is only one road."

The ground was carpeted with flowers which were all alike: they were snow-white pansies and very pretty; but, as they never saw the sun, they had no scent.

And, as they walked along, the Children gathered a beautiful white nosegay. The dear little things did not know that every pansy (which means "a thought") that they picked brought them nearer to their grandparents; and they soon saw before them a large oak with a notice-board nailed to it.

"Here we are!" cried the boy in triumph, as, climbing up on a root, he read:

"The Land of Memory."

They had arrived; but they turned to every side without seeing a thing: "I can see nothing at all!" whimpered Mytyl. "I'm cold! I'm tired··· I don't want to travel anymore!" At present, Tyltyl cried with excitement: "There! Look! Look! The fog is lifting!"

And, sure enough, the mist parted before their eyes, like veils

torn by an invisible hand; the big trees faded away and, instead, there appeared a pretty little peasant's cottage, covered with creepers and standing in a little garden filled with flowers and with trees all over fruit.

The Children at once knew the dear cow in the orchard, the watch-dog at the door, the blackbird in his wicker cage; and everything was steeped in a pale light and a warm and balmy air.

Tyltyl and Mytyl stood amazed. So that was the Land of Memory! They at once made up their minds to come back often, now that they knew the way. But how great was their happiness when the last veil disappeared and they saw, at a few steps from them, Grandad and Granny sitting on a bench, sound asleep. They called out gleefully:

"It's Grandad! It's Granny! There they are! There they are!"

Then they heard Granny trembling voice say: "I have a notion that our grandchildren who are still alive are coming to see us today."

And Grandad answered: "They are certainly thinking of us, for I feel queer and I have pins and needles in my legs⋯"

Grandad had not time to finish sentence. The Children were in Granny's and Grandad's arms! What wild kisses and huggings! What a wonderful surprise! The happiness was too great for words. It was so glorious and so unexpected to meet again like this.

"How tall and strong you've grown, Tyltyl!" said Granny.

And Grandad cried: "And Mytyl! Just look at her! What pretty hair, what pretty eyes!"

And the Children danced and clapped their hands and flung themselves by turns into the arms of one or the other.

At last, they quieted down a little; and, with Mytyl nestling against Grandad's chest and Tyltyl comfortably perched on Granny's knees,

they began to talk of family affairs: "How are Daddy and Mummy?" asked Granny.

"Quite well, Granny," said Tyltyl. "They were asleep when we went out."

Granny gave them fresh kisses and said: "My word, how pretty they are and how nice and clean! Why don't you come to see us oftener? It is months and months now that you have forgotten us and that we have seen nobody…"

"We couldn't, Granny," said Tyltyl, "and today it's only because of the Fairy…"

"We are always here," said Granny, "waiting for a visit from those who are alive. The last time you were here was on All-hallows…"

"All-hallows? We didn't go out that day, for we both had colds!"

"But you thought of us! And, every time you think of us, we wake up and see you again."

Tyltyl's head on the heart of the dear Granny whom he had missed so much, he began to understand things and he felt that his grandparents had not left him altogether. He asked: "So you are not really dead?"

The old couple burst out laughing. When they exchanged their life on earth for another and a much nicer and more beautiful life, they had forgotten the word "dead."

"What does that word 'dead' mean?" asked Grandad.

"Why, it means that one's no longer alive!" said Tyltyl.

Grandad and Granny only shrugged their shoulders: "How stupid the Living are, when they speak of the Others!" was all they

said.

Tyltyl had jumped off Granny's knees and was poking about in every corner, delighted at finding all sorts of things which he knew and remembered: "Nothing is changed, everything is in its old place!" he cried. And, as he had not been to the old people's home for so long, everything struck him as much nicer; and he added, in the voice of one who knows, "Only everything is prettier! Look, there's the clock with the big hand which I broke the point off and the hole which I made in the door, the day I found Grandad's gimlet⋯"

"Yes, you've done some damage in your time!" said Grandad.

"And there's the plum tree which you were so fond of climbing, when I wasn't looking⋯"

Meantime, Tyltyl was not forgetting his errand: "You haven't the Blue Bird here by chance, I suppose?"

At the same moment, Mytyl, lifting her head, saw a cage: "Look, there's the old blackbird! Does he still sing?"

As she spoke, the blackbird woke up and began to sing at the top of his voice.

"You see," said Granny, "as soon as one thinks of him⋯"

Tyltyl was simply amazed at what he saw: "But he's blue!" he shouted. "Why, that's the bird, the Blue Bird! He's blue, blue, blue as a blue glass marble! Will you give him to me?"

The grandparents gladly consented; and, full of triumph, Tyltyl went and fetched the cage which he had left by the tree. He took hold of the precious bird with the greatest of care; and it began to hop around in its new home.

"How pleased the Fairy will be!" said the boy, rejoicing at his conquest. "And Light too!"

The children suddenly asked if their little dead brothers and sisters were there too. At the same moment, seven little children, who, up to then, had been sleeping in the house, came tearing like mad into the garden. Tyltyl and Mytyl ran up to them. They all hustled and hugged one another and danced and whirled about and uttered screams of joy.

"Here they are, here they are!" said Granny. "As soon as you speak of them, they are there, the imps!"

Tyltyl caught a little one by the hair: "Pierrot! So we're going to fight again, as in the old days! And Robert! I say, Jean, what's become of your top? Madeleine and Pierrette and Pauline··· And here's Riquette!"

Mytyl laughed: "Riquette's still crawling on all fours!"

Tyltyl noticed a little dog yapping around them: "There's Kiki, whose tail I cut off with Pauline's scissors··· He hasn't changed either."

"No," said Grandad, in a voice of great importance, "nothing changes here!"

But, suddenly, amid the general rejoicings, the old people stopped spell-bound: they had heard the small voice of the clock indoors strike eight!

"How's this?" they asked. "It never strikes nowadays··· Was anyone thinking of the time?"

"Yes, I was," said Tyltyl. "So it's eight o' clock? Then I'm off, for I promised Light to be back before nine···"

He was going for the cage, but the others were too happy to let him run away so soon: it would be horrid to say goodbye like that! Granny knew what a little glutton Tyltyl was. It was just supper-time

and, as luck would have it, there was some capital cabbage soup and a beautiful plum-tart.

"Well," said Tyltyl, "as I've got the Blue Bird! And cabbage soup is a thing you don't have every day!"

They all hurried and carried the table outside and laid it with a nice white table-cloth and put a plate for each; and, lastly, Granny brought out the steaming soup-tureen in state. The lamp was lit and the grandparents and grandchildren sat down to supper, jostling and elbowing one another and laughing and shouting with pleasure.

Then, for a time, nothing was heard but the sound of the wooden spoons noisily clattering against the soup-plates.

"How good it is! Oh, how good it is!" shouted Tyltyl, who was eating greedily. "I want some more! More! More! More!"

"Come, come, a little more quiet," said Grandad. "You're just as ill-behaved as ever; and you'll break your plate···"

Tyltyl took no notice of the remark, stood up on his stool, caught hold of the tureen and dragged it towards him and upset it; and the hot soup trickled all over the table and down upon everybody's lap. The children yelled and screamed with pain. Granny was quite scared; and Grandad was furious. He dealt Tyltyl a tremendous box on the ear.

Tyltyl was staggered for a moment; and then he put his hand to his cheek with a look of rapture and exclaimed: "Grandad, how good, how jolly! It was just like the slaps you used to give me when you were alive! I must give you a kiss for it!"

Everybody laughed.

"There's more where that came from, if you like them!" said Grandad, grumpily. But he was touched, all the same, and turned to wipe a tear from his eyes.

"Goodness!" cried Tyltyl, starting up. "There's half-past eight striking! Mytyl, we've only just got time!"

Granny in vain implored them to stay a few minutes longer.

"No, we can't possibly," said Tyltyl firmly; "I promised Light!"

And he hurried to take up the precious cage.

"Goodbye, Grandad··· Goodbye, Granny. Goodbye, brothers and sisters, Pierrot, Robert, Pauline, Madeleine, Riquette and you, too, Kiki... We can't stay··· Don't cry, Granny; we will come back often!"

"Come back every day!" said Granny. "It is our only pleasure; and it's such a treat for us when your thoughts pay us a visit!"

"Goodbye! Goodbye!" cried the brothers and sisters in chorus. "Come back very soon! Bring us some barley sugar!"

There were more kisses; all waved their handkerchiefs; all shouted a last goodbye. But the figures began to fade away; the little voices could no longer be heard; the two Children were once more wrapped in mist; and the old forest covered them with its great dark mantle.

"I'm so frightened!" whimpered Mytyl. "Give me your hand, little brother! I'm so frightened!"

Tyltyl was shaking too, but it was his duty to try and comfort and console his sister: "Hush!" he said. "Remember that we are bringing back the Blue Bird!"

As he spoke, a thin ray of light pierced the gloom; and the little boy hurried towards it. He was holding his cage tight in his arms; and the first thing he did was to look at his bird···Alas and alack, what a disappointment! The beautiful Blue Bird of the Land of Memory had turned quite black! Stare at it as hard as Tyltyl might, the bird was black! Oh, how well he knew the old blackbird that used to sing in its wicker prison, in the old days, at the door of the house! What had

happened? How painful it was! And how cruel life seemed to him just then!

To add to his misfortunes, he could not find the straight road by which he had come. There was not a single white pansy on the ground; and he began to cry.

Luckily, the Fairy had promised that Light would watch over them. The mist suddenly lifted again. But, instead of disclosing the old people's house, it revealed a marvelous temple, with a blinding glare streaming from it.

On the threshold stood Light, fair and beautiful in her diamond-colored dress. She smiled when Tyltyl told her of his first failure. She knew everything. For Light surrounds all mortals with her love, though none of them is fond enough of her ever to, receive her thoroughly and thus to learn all the secrets of Truth.

She was going to try and conquer a human soul: "Do not be sad," she said to the Children. "Are you not pleased to have seen your grandparents? Is that not enough happiness for one day? Are you not glad to have restored the old blackbird to life? Listen to him singing!"

For the old blackbird was singing with might and main; and his little yellow eyes sparkled with pleasure as he hopped about his big cage.

"As you-look for the Blue Bird, dear Children, accustom yourselves to love the grey birds which you find on your way."

It was quite clear that Light knew where the Blue Bird was. But life is often full of beautiful mysteries, which we must respect, lest we should destroy them; and, if Light had told the Children where the Blue Bird was, well, they would never have found him! And our little friends slept on beautiful white clouds under Light's watchful care.

4

THE PALACE OF NIGHT

At dawn, the Children and their friends went to the Palace of Night, where they hoped to find the Blue Bird. Milk and Water both sent an excuse to ask for absence. As for Light, she had been on bad terms with Night since the world began; and Fire shared her dislike as a relation. Light kissed the Children and told Tylo the way, because it was his responsibility to lead the expedition. And then the little band set out upon its road.

Tylo was trotting ahead, on his hindlegs, like a little man. He was joining blindly in his little gods' search, without for a moment reflecting that the end of the journey would mean the end of his life.

"Ah," he said, "if I got hold of that rascal of a Blue Bird, trust me, I wouldn't touch him even with the tip of my tongue, not if he were as plump and sweet as a quail!"

Bread followed solemnly, carrying the cage; the two Children came next; and Sugar brought up the rear.

But where was the Cat?

"The idiots," Cat thought, "have very nearly spoiled the whole thing. It is better to rely upon one's self alone." She resolved to act before daybreak, to call on Night, who was an old friend of hers.

The Cat raced along the road, light as a feather. Her cloak, borne on the wind, streamed like a banner behind her; the plume in her hat

fluttered gracefully; and her little grey kid boots hardly touched the ground. She soon reached her destination and, in a few bounds, came to the great hall where Night was.

It was really a wonderful sight. Night, stately and grand as a Queen, reclined upon her throne; she slept; and not a glimmer, not a star twinkled around her. But the night has no secrets for cats and their eyes have the power of piercing the darkness. So Tylette saw Night as though it were broad daylight.

Before waking her, she cast a loving glance at that motherly and familiar face. It was white and silvery as the moon; and its unbending features inspired both fear and admiration. Night's figure, which was half visible through her long black veils, was as beautiful as that of a Greek statue. She had no arms and a pair of enormous wings, now furled in sleep, came from her shoulders to her feet and gave her a look of majesty beyond compare.

"It is I, Mother Night! I am worn out!"

Night is of an anxious nature and easily alarmed. Her beauty, built up of peace and repose, possesses the secret of Silence. A star shooting through the sky, a leaf falling to the ground, the hoot of an owl, a mere nothing is enough to tear the black velvet pall which she spreads over the earth each evening. Her immense wings beat around her; and she questioned Tylette in a trembling voice. What! A man's son coming to her palace! And, perhaps, with the help of the magic diamond, discovering her secrets!

"I see only one thing for it, Mother Night. As they are children, we must give them such a fright that they will not dare to insist on opening the great door at the back of the hall, behind which the Birds of the Moon live and generally the Blue Bird too. The secrets of the other caverns will be sure to scare them. The hope of our safety lies in the terror which you will make them feel." the Cat explained this plan to Night in a few words.

There was clearly no other course to take. But Night had no time to reply, for she heard a sound. Then her beautiful features contracted; her wings spread out angrily; and everything in her attitude told Tylette that Night approved of her plan.

"Here they are!" cried the Cat.

The little band came marching down the steps of Night's gloomy staircase. Picture a huge and wonderful black marble hall, of a stem and tomb-like splendor. There is no ceiling visible; and the ebony pillars that surround the amphitheater shoot up to the sky. It is only when you lift your eyes up there that you catch the faint light falling from the stars. Everywhere, the thickest darkness reigns. Two restless flames flicker on either side of Night's throne, before a monumental door of brass. Bronze doors show through the pillars to the right and left.

The Cat rushed up to the Children: "This way, little master, this way! I have told Night; and she is delighted to see you." Tyltyl walked up to the throne with a bold and confident step. He very gently asked for permission to look for the Blue Bird in her palace.

"I have never seen him, he is not here!" exclaimed Night, flapping her great wings to frighten the boy.

But, when Tyltyl insisted and gave no sign of fear, she herself began to dread the diamond, which, by lighting up her darkness, would completely destroy her power; and she thought it better to pretend to yield to an impulse of generosity and at once to point to the big key that lay on the steps of the throne.

Without a moment's hesitation, Tyltyl seized hold of it and ran to the first door of the hall.

Everybody shook with fright. Meanwhile, Tyltyl, pale and resolute, was trying to open the door, while Night's grave voice, rising above the din, proclaimed the first danger.

"It's the Ghosts!"

The faithful Tylo, by his side, was

140

panting with all his might, for dogs hate anything uncanny.

At last, the key grated in the lock. No one dared draw a breath. In a moment, the gloom was filled with white figures running in every direction. Some lengthened out right up to the sky; others twined themselves round the pillars; others wriggled ever so fast along the ground. They were moving so fast that it was impossible to distinguish their features. Tyltyl did his best to chase them; for Mrs. Night pretended to be frightened. She had been the Ghosts' friend for hundreds and hundreds of years and had only to say a word to drive them in again; but she was flapping her wings like mad, she called upon all her gods and screamed: "Drive them away! Drive them away! Help! Help!"

But the poor Ghosts, who hardly ever come out now that Man no longer believes in them, were much too happy at taking a breath of air; and, had it not been that they were afraid of Tylo, who tried to bite their legs, they would never have been put back indoors.

"Oof!" gasped the Dog, when the door was shut at last. "I have strong teeth, goodness knows. When you bite them, you'd think their legs were made of cotton!"

By this time, Tyltyl was walking toward the second door and asking: "What's behind this one? Must I be careful when I open it?"

"No," said Night, "it is not worthwhile. It's the Sicknesses. They are very quiet, the poor little things! Man, for some time, has been waging such war upon them! Open and see for yourself."

Tyltyl threw the door wide open and there was nothing to be seen. He was just about to close the door again, when he was hustled aside by a little body in a dressing-gown and a cotton night-cap, who began to frisk about the hall, wagging her head and stopping every

minute to cough, sneeze and blow her nose··· and to pull on her slippers, which were too big for her and kept dropping off her feet. Sugar, Bread and Tyltyl were no longer frightened and began to laugh like anything. But they had no sooner Come near the little person in the cotton night-cap than they themselves began to cough and sneeze.

"It's the least important of the Sicknesses," said Night. "It's Cold."

"Oh, dear, oh, dear!" thought Sugar. "If my nose keeps on running like this, I'm done for: I shall melt!" Poor Sugar! He did not know where to hide himself. Sugar would have had to fly from the palace, but for the timely aid of our dear Tylo, who ran after the little girl and drove her back to her cavern, amidst the laughter of Tyltyl and Mytyl, who thought gleefully that the trial had not been very terrible so far.

Therefore, the boy ran to the next door with still greater courage.

"Take care!" cried Night, in a dreadful voice. "It's the Wars! They are more powerful than ever! I dare not think what would happen, if one of them broke loose! Stand ready, all of you, to push back the door!"

Night had not finished uttering her warnings, when the plucky little fellow repented his rashness. He tried in vain to shut the door which he had opened: an invincible force was pushing it from the other side , streams of blood flowed through the cracks; flames shot forth; shouts, oaths and groans mingled with the roar of cannon and the rattle of musketry. Everybody in the Palace of Night was running about in wild confusion. Bread and Sugar tried to take to flight, but could not find the way out; and they now came back to Tyltyl and put their shoulders to the door with despairing force.

The Cat pretended to be anxious, while secretly rejoicing:

"This may be the end of it," she said, curling her whiskers. "They won't dare to go on after this."

Dear Tylo made superhuman efforts to help his little master, while Mytyl stood crying in a corner.

At last, Tyltyl gave a shout of triumph: "Hurray! They're giving way! Victory! Victory! The door is shut!" At the same time, he dropped on the steps, utterly exhausted, dabbing his forehead with his poor little hands which shook with terror.

"Well?" asked Night, harshly. "Have you had enough? Did you see them?"

"Yes, yes!" replied the little fellow, sobbing. "They are hideous and awful⋯ I don't think they have the Blue Bird."

"You may be sure they haven't," answered Night, angrily. "If they had, they would eat him at once. You see there is nothing to be done."

Tyltyl drew himself up proudly: "I must see everything," he declared. "Light said so."

"It's an easy thing to say," retorted Night, "when one's afraid and stays at home!"

"Let us go to the next door," said Tyltyl, resolutely. "What's in here?"

"Do not open that one!" said Night, in awe-struck tones.

"Why not?"

"Because it's not allowed!"

"Then it's here that the Blue Bird is hidden!"

"Go no farther, do not tempt fate, do not open that door!"

"But why?" again asked Tyltyl, obstinately.

Thereupon, Night, irritated by his persistency, flew into a rage, hurled the most terrible threats at him, and ended by saying:

"Not one of those who have opened it has ever returned alive to the light of day! It means certain death; and all the horrors, all the terrors, all the fears of which men speak on earth are as nothing compared with those which await you if you insist on touching that door!"

"Don't do it, master dear!" said Bread, with chattering teeth. "Don't do it! Take pity on us! I implore you on my knees!"

"You are sacrificing the lives of all of us," mewed the Cat.

"I won't! I shall not!" sobbed Mytyl.

"Pity! Pity!" whined Sugar, wringing his fingers.

All of them were weeping and crying, all of them crowded round Tyltyl. Dear Tylo alone, who respected his little master's wishes, dared not speak a word, though he fully believed that his last hour had come. Two big tears rolled down his cheeks; and he licked Tyltyl's hands in despair. And for a moment, Tyltyl hesitated. His heart beat wildly. He did not wish to show weakness in the presence of his hapless companions! "If I have not the strength to fulfil my task," he said to himself, "who will fulfil it? If my friends behold my distress, it is all up with me: they will not let me go through with my mission and I shall never find the Blue Bird!"

Tyltyl resolved to sacrifice himself. He brandished the heavy golden key and cried: "I must open the door!"

He ran up to the great door, with Tylo panting by his side. The poor Dog was half-dead with fright, but his pride and his devotion to Tyltyl obliged him to smother his fears: "I shall stay," he said to his master, "I'm not afraid! I shall stay with my little god!"

In the meantime, all the others had fled. Bread was crumbling to bits behind a pillar; Sugar was melting in a corner with Mytyl in his arms; Night and the Cat, both shaking with fury, kept to the far end of the hall.

Then Tyltyl gave Tylo a last kiss, pressed him to his heart and put the key in the lock with no tremble. Yells of terror came from all the corners of the hall, where the runaways had taken shelter, while the two leaves of the great door opened by magic in front of Tyltyl, who was struck dumb with admiration and delight. What an exquisite surprise! A wonderful garden lay before him, a dream garden filled with flowers that shone like stars, waterfalls that came rushing from the sky and trees which the moon had clothed in silver. And then there was something whirling like a blue cloud among the clusters of roses. Tyltyl rubbed his eyes; he could not believe his senses. He waited, looked again and then dashed into the garden, shouting like mad:

"Come quickly! Come quickly! They are here! We have them at last! Millions of blue birds! Thousands of millions! Come, Mytyl! Come, Tylo! Come, all! Help me! You can catch them by handfuls!"

Reassured at last, his friends came running up and all darted in among the birds, seeing who could catch the most:

"I've caught seven already!" cried Mytyl. "I can't hold them!"

"Nor can I!" said Tyltyl. "I have too many of them! They're escaping from my arms! Tylo has some too! Let us go out, let us go! Light is waiting for us! How pleased she will be! This way, this way!"

And they all danced and scampered away in their glee, singing songs of triumph as they went.

Night and the Cat, who had not shared in the general rejoicing, crept back anxiously to the great door; and Night whimpered: "Haven't they got him?"

"No," said the Cat, who saw the real Blue Bird perched high up on a moonbeam. "They could not reach him, he kept too high."

They in all haste ran up the numberless stairs between them and the daylight. Each of them hugged the birds which he had captured. By the time they came to the top of the staircase, they were carrying nothing but dead birds.

Light was waiting for them anxiously: "Well, have you caught him?" she asked.

"Yes, yes!" said Tyltyl. "Lots of them! There are thousands! Look!"

As he spoke, to his dismay, he saw that Blue Birds' poor little wings were broken and their heads drooped sadly from their necks! The boy turned to his companions. Alas, they too were hugging nothing but dead birds!

Then Tyltyl threw himself sobbing into Light's arms. Once more, all his hopes were dashed to the ground.

"Do not cry, my child," said Light. "You did not catch the one that is able to live in broad daylight. We shall find him yet."

"Of course, we shall find him," said Bread and Sugar, with one voice. They wanted to console the boy. As for friend Tylo, he was so much put out that he forgot his dignity for a moment and, looking at the dead birds, exclaimed: "Are they good to eat, I wonder?"

The party set out to walk back and sleep in the Temple of Light.

Sugar edged up to Bread and whispered in his ear: "Don't you think, Mr. Chairman, that all this excitement is very useless?"

And Bread, who felt flattered at receiving so much attention, answered, pompously: "Never you fear, my dear fellow. Life would be unbearable if we had to listen to all the whimsies of that little madcap! Tomorrow, we shall stay in bed!"

Meanwhile, the party walked on, the Temple of Light stood on a crystal height, shedding its beams around. The tired Children made the Dog carry them pick-a-back by turns; and they were almost asleep when they reached the shining steps.

5

THE KINGDOM OF THE FUTURE

All the Animals and Things had all met in the underground vaults of the temple. Light knew that, if they were left to do as they pleased, they might escape and get into mischief. This great hall had sofas in it and a gold table laid with fruits and cakes and creams and delicious wines, which Light's servants had just finished setting out. Nothing amused Animals and Things more than eating and sleeping and that they were very glad to stay where they were. Except Tylo, but Light told him that fate would soon provide a trial for the Children in which his assistance would be of great use.

As she spoke these words, she touched the emerald wall, which opened to let her pass through with the Children.

Her chariot was waiting outside the entrance to the temple. It was a lovely shell of jade, inlaid with gold. They all three took their seats; and the two great white birds harnessed to it at once flew off through

the clouds. The chariot travelled very fast; and the Children, who were enjoying themselves and laughing like anything.

The clouds vanished around them; and, suddenly, they found themselves in a dazzling azure palace. Here, all was blue: the light, the flagstones, the columns, the vaults; everything, down to the smallest objects, was of an intense and fairy-like blue. There was no seeing the end of the palace; the eyes were lost in the infinite sapphire vistas.

"How lovely it all is!" said Tyltyl, who could not get over his astonishment. "Goodness me, how lovely! Where are we?"

"We are in the Kingdom of the Future," said Light, "in the midst of the children who are not yet born. We shall perhaps find the Blue Bird here. Look! Look at the children running up!"

From every side came bands of little children dressed from head to foot in blue; they had beautiful dark or golden hair and they were all exquisitely pretty. They shouted gleefully:

"Live Children! Come and look at the little Live Children!"

"What a lot there are! What a lot there are!" cried Tyltyl.

"There are many more," said Light. "No one could count them. But go a little further: you will see other things."

Tyltyl did as he was told and elbowed his way through; but it was difficult for him to

move, because a crowd of Blue Children pressed all around them. At last, by mounting on a step, our little friend was able to look over the throng of inquisitive heads and see what was happening in every part of the hall. It was most extraordinary! Tyltyl had never dreamed of anything like it! He danced with joy; and Mytyl, who was hanging on to him and standing on tiptoe so that she might see too, clapped her little hands and gave loud cries of wonder.

All around were millions of Children in blue, some playing, others walking about, others talking or thinking. Many were asleep; many also were at work; and their instruments, their tools, the machines which they were building, the plants, the flowers and the fruits which they were growing or gathering were of the same bright and heavenly blue as the general appearance of the palace.

One of them stood close to Tyltyl. He was quite small. From under his long sky blue silk dress peeped two little pink and dimpled bare feet. His eyes stared in curiosity at the little Live Boy; and he went up to him as though in spite of himself.

"How do you do?" said Tyltyl, putting out his hand to the Child.

But the Child did not understand what that meant and stood without moving.

The Child, who was absorbed in what he was looking at, gravely touched Tyltyl's hat with his finger:

"And that?" he lisped.

"That... That's my hat," said Tyltyl. "Have you no hat?"

"No; what is it for?" asked the Child.

"It's to say How-do-you-do with," Tyltyl answered. "And then for when it's cold..."

"What does that mean, when it's cold?" asked the Child.

"When you shiver like this: Brrr! Brrrl" said Tyltyl. "And when you go like this with your arms," vigorously beating his arms across his chest.

"Is it cold on earth?" asked the Child.

"Yes, sometimes, in winter, when there is no fire."

"Why is there no fire?"

"Because it's expensive; and it costs money to buy wood."

The Child looked at Tyltyl again as though he did not understand a word that Tyltyl was saying; and Tyltyl in his turn looked amazed.

"How old are you?" asked Tyltyl.

"I am going to be born soon," said the Child. "I shall be born in twelve years. Is it nice to be born?"

"Oh, yes," cried Tyltyl, without thinking. "It's great fun!"

"They say it's lovely, the earth and the Live People!" remarked the Child.

"Yes, it's not bad," said Tyltyl. "There are birds and cakes and toys. Some have them all; but those who have none can look at the others!"

Tytyl had never felt depressed for his poverty but enjoyed the good fortune of others.

The two Children talked a good deal more. At that moment, a great breath of wind made him turn his head and he saw, at a few steps away from him, a large piece of machinery. It was a grand and magnificent thing, but had no name yet, because the inventions of the Kingdom of the Future will not be christened by Man until they reach the earth. When Tyltyl looked at it, he thought that the enormous azure wings that whizzed so swiftly before his eyes were like the

windmills in his part of the world and that, if he ever found the Blue Bird, its wings would certainly be no more delicate, dainty or dazzling. Full of admiration, he asked his new acquaintance what they were.

"Those?" said the Child. "That's for the invention which I shall make on earth."

And, seeing Tyltyl stare with wide-open eyes, he added:

"When I am on earth, I shall have to invent the thing that gives happiness. Would you like to see it? It is over there, between those two columns."

Tyltyl turned round to look; but all the Children at once rushed at him, shouting:

"No, no, come and see mine!"

"No, mine is much finer!"

"Mine is a wonderful invention!"

"Mine is made of sugar!"

"His is no good!"

"I'm bringing a light which nobody knows of!"

And, so saying, the last Child lit himself up entirely with a most extraordinary flame.

Amid these joyous exclamations, the Live Children were dragged towards the blue Workshops, where each of the little inventors set his machine going. It was a great blue whirl of disks and pulleys and straps and fly-wheels and driving-wheels and cog-wheels and all kinds of wheels, which sent every sort of machine skimming over the ground or shooting up to the ceiling. Other Blue Children unfolded maps and plans, or opened great big books, or uncovered azure statues, or brought enormous flowers and gigantic fruits that seemed made of sapphires and turquoises.

Our little friends stood with their mouths wide open and their hands clasped together: they thought themselves in paradise. Mytyl bent over to look at a huge flower and laughed into its cup, which covered up her head like a hood of blue silk. A pretty Child, with dark hair and thoughtful eyes, held it by the stalk and said, proudly:

"The flowers will all grow like that, when I am on earth!"

Next came another Child came along almost hidden under a basket which one of the tall persons was helping him to carry. His fair-haired, rosy face smiled through the leaves that hung over the wicker-work.

"Look!" he said. "Look at my apples."

"But those are melons!" said Tyltyl.

"No, no!" said the Child. "They are my apples! They will all be alike when I am alive! I have discovered the process!"

Tyltyl was eager to know as many more of the Children as he could. He was introduced to the discoverer of a new sun, to the inventor of a new joy, to the hero who was to wipe out injustice from the earth and to the wiseacre who was to conquer Death. There were such lots and lots of them that it would take days and days to name them all. He was rather tired and was beginning to feel bored, when his attention was suddenly aroused by hearing a Child's voice calling him:

"Tyltyl! Tyltyl! How are you, Tyltyl, how are you?"

A little Blue Child came running up from the back of the hall, pushing his way through the crowd. He was fair and slim and bright-eyed and had a great look of Mytyl.

"How do you know my name?" asked Tyltyl.

"It's not surprising," said the Blue Child, "considering that I shall be your brother!"

This time, the Live Children were absolutely amazed. What an extraordinary meeting! They must certainly tell Mummy as soon as they got back! How astonished they would be at home!

The Child went on to explain: "I am coming to you next year, on Palm Sunday," he said.

And he put a thousand questions to his big brother: was it comfortable at home? Was the food good? Was Daddy very severe? And Mummy?

"Oh, Mummy is so kind!" said the little ones.

And they asked him questions in their turn: what was he going to do on earth? What was he bringing?

"I am bringing three illnesses," said the little brother. "Scarlatina, whooping-cough and measles."

"Oh, why?" cried Tyltyl. He shook his head, with evident disappointment.

"After that, I shall leave you!" the future Brother continued.

"It will hardly be worthwhile coming!" said Tyltyl, feeling rather vexed.

"We can't pick and choose!" said the little brother, pettishly.

They would perhaps have quarrelled, without waiting till they were on earth, if they had not suddenly been parted by a swarm of Blue Children who were hurrying to meet somebody. At the same time, there was a great noise, as if thousands of invisible doors were being opened at the end of the galleries.

"What's the matter?" asked Tyltyl.

"It's Time," said one of the Blue Children. "He's going to open the doors."

And the excitement increased on every side. The Children left their machines and their labors; those who were asleep woke up; and every eye was eagerly and anxiously turned to the great opal doors at the back, while every mouth repeated the same name. The word,

"Time! Time!" was heard all around; and the great mysterious noise kept on. Tyltyl was dying to know what it meant. At last, he caught a little Child by the skirt of his dress and asked him.

"Let me be," said the Child, very uneasily. "I'm in a hurry it may be my turn today. It is the Dawn rising. This is the hour when the Children who are to be born today go down to earth. You shall see. Time is drawing the bolts."

"Who is Time?" asked Tyltyl.

"An old man who comes to call those who are going," said another Child. "He is not so bad; but he won't listen or hear. Beg as they may, if it's not their turn, he pushes back all those who try to go. Let me be! It may be my turn now!"

Light now hastened towards our little friends in a great state of alarm:

"I was looking for you," she said. "Come quick: it will never do for Time to discover you."

As she spoke these words, she threw her gold cloak around the Children and dragged them to a corner of the hall, where they could see everything, without being seen.

Tyltyl was very glad to be so well protected. He now knew that he who was about to appear possessed so great and tremendous a power that no human strength was capable of resisting him. He was at the same time a deity and an ogre; he bestowed life and he devoured it; he sped through the world so fast that you had no time to see him; he ate and ate, without stopping; he took whatever he touched. In Tyltyl's family, he had already taken Grandad and Granny, the little brothers, the little sisters and the old blackbird. He did not mind what he took: joys and sorrows, winters and summers, all was fish that came to his net!

Knowing this, Tyltyl was astonished to see everybody in the Kingdom of the Future running so fast to meet him. "I suppose he doesn't eat anything here," he thought.

There he was! The great doors turned slowly on their hinges. There was a distant music: it was the sounds of the earth. A red and green light penetrated into the hall; and Time appeared on the threshold. He was a tall and very thin old man, so old that his wrinkled face was all grey, like dust. His white beard came down to his knees. In one hand, he carried an enormous scythe; in the other, an hour-glass. Behind him; some way out, on a sea the color of the Dawn, was a magnificent gold galley, with white sails.

"Are they ready whose hour has struck?" asked Time. At the sound of that voice, solemn and deep as a bronze gong, thousands of bright children's voices, like little silver bells, answered:

"Here we are! Here we are! Here we are!"

And, in a moment, the Blue Children were crowding round the tall old man, who pushed them all back and, in a gruff voice, said:

"One at a time! Once again, there are many more of you than are wanted! You can't deceive me!"

Brandishing his scythe in one hand and holding out his cloak with the other, he barred the way to the rash Children who tried to slip by him. Not one of them escaped the horrid old man's watchful eye:

"It's not your turn!" he said to one. "You're to be born tomorrow! Nor yours either, you've gotten years to wait. A thirteenth shepherd? There are only twelve wanted; there is no need for more. More doctors? There are too many already; they are grumbling about it on earth. And where are the engineers? They want an honest man; only one, as a wonderful being."

And the movement went on. Each Child, when denied, returned to his employment with a downcast air. When one of them was accepted, the others looked at him with envy. Now and then, something happened, as when the hero who was to fight against injustice refused to go. He clung to his playfellows, who called out to Time:

"He doesn't want to, Sir!"

"No, I don't want to go," cried the little fellow, with all his might. "I would rather not be born."

"And quite right too!" thought Tyltyl, who was full of common sense and who knew what things are like on earth.

For people always get beatings which they have not deserved; and, when they have done wrong, you may be sure that the punishment will fall on one of their innocent friends.

"I wouldn't care to be in his place," said Tyltyl to himself. "I would rather hunt for the Blue Bird, any day!"

Meanwhile, the little seeker after justice went away sobbing, frightened out of his life by Mr. Time.

The excitement was now at its height. The Children ran all over the hall: those who were going packed up their inventions.

Time, in a huge voice, shaking his big keys and his terrible scythe, roared: "The anchor's weighed."

Then the Children climbed into the gold galley, with the beautiful white silk sails. They waved their hands again to the little friends whom they were leaving behind them; but, on seeing the earth in the distance, they cried out, gladly:

"Earth! Earth! I can see it!"

"How bright it is!"

"How big it is!"

And, at the same time, as though coming from the abyss, a song rose, a distant song of gladness and expectation.

Light, who was listening with a smile, saw the look of astonishment on Tyltyl's face and bent over him:

"It is the song of the mothers coming out to meet them," she said.

At that moment, Time, who had shut the doors, saw our friends and rushed at them angrily, shaking his scythe at them.

"Hurry!" said Light. "Hurry! Take the Blue Bird, Tyltyl, and go in front of me with Mytyl."

She put into the boy's arms a bird which she held hidden under her cloak and, all radiant, spreading her dazzling veil with her two hands, she ran on, protecting her charges from the onslaught of Time.

In this way, they passed through several turquoise and sapphire galleries. It was magnificently beautiful, but they were in the Kingdom of the Future, where Time was the great master, and they must escape from his anger which they had braved.

Mytyl was terribly frightened and Tyltyl kept nervously turning round to Light.

"Don't be afraid," she said. "Only mind that you take care of the Blue Bird. He's gorgeous! He is quite, quite blue!"

This thought enraptured the boy. He felt the precious treasure fluttering in his arms; his hands dared not press the pretty creature's soft, warm wings; and his heart beat against its heart.

They were just about to cross the threshold of the palace, when a gust of wind swept through the entrance hall, lifting up Light's veil and at last revealing the two Children to the eyes of Time, who was

still pursuing them. With a roar of rage, he darted his scythe at Tyltyl, who cried out. Light warded off the blow; and the door of the palace closed behind them with a thud. They were saved! But alas, Tyltyl, taken by surprise, had opened his arms and now, through his tears, saw the Bird of the Future soaring above their heads, mingling with the azure sky its dream-wings so blue, so light and so transparent that soon the boy could make out nothing more⋯

6

THE PALACE OF
HAPPINESS

Next morning, Light told Tyltyl and Mytyl that they need to leave for the Palace of Happiness.

"This time, I believe we can find the Blue Bird."

They walked to an extremely elegant hall. The architecture suggested the most sensual and sumptuous moments of the Venetian or Flemish Renascence. In the middle stands a massive and marvelous table of jasper and silver-gilt, laden with candlesticks, glass, gold and silver plate and fabulous viands. Around the table, the biggest luxuries of the Earth sat eating, drinking, shouting, singing, tossing and lolling around or sleeping among the haunches of venison, the miraculous fruits, the overturned jars and ewers. They were enormously, incredibly fat and red in the face, covered with velvet and brocade, crowned with gold and pearls and precious stones. Beautiful female slaves incessantly brought decorated dishes and foaming beverages. Vulgar, blatantly hilarious music, in which the brasses predominated. The forefront of the palace was bathed in a red and heavy light.

Tyltyl, Mytyl, the Dog, Bread and Sugar were little awestruck at first and crowd round Light. The Cat, without a word, walked to the other side of the hall, lifted a dark valance and disappears.

"Who are those fat gentlemen enjoying themselves and eating such a lot of good things?" asked Tyltyl to Light.

"They are the biggest Luxuries of the Earth. It is possible, though not very likely, that the Blue Bird may have strayed among them for a moment. That is why you must not turn the diamond yet. For form's sake, we will begin by searching this part of the hall." Light answered.

"Can we go up to them?"

"Certainly. They are not ill-natured, although they are vulgar and usually rather ill-bred."

"What beautiful cakes they have!" said Mytyl with admiration and looked at those cakes and candies.

"And such game! And sausages! And legs of lamb and calves' liver!" Tylo couldn't help but also exclaimed. "There is nothing nicer or lovelier in the world than liver!"

A dozen of the biggest Luxuries had risen from table and held their stomachs in their hands, advance laboriously towards the Children. Tyltyl then quick backed to Light.

"Have no fear, they are very affable... They will probably invite you to dinner... Do not accept anything. They are dangerous and would break your will." Light comforted the Children.

"What? Not even a tiny cake? They look so good, so fresh, so well iced with sugar, covered with candied fruits and brimming over with cream!" Tyltyl felt confused.

The biggest of the Luxuries held out his hand to Tyltyl and said: "I am the Luxury of Being Rich; and I come, in the name of my brothers, to beg you and your family to honor our endless repast with your presence." Then he seized Tyltyl's hands, "Please come along! They are beginning the banquet all over again... We are only waiting for you... Do you hear all the revelers calling and shouting for you? I cannot introduce you to all of them, there are so many of them... Allow me to lead you to the two seats of honor."

"No, thank you very much, Mr. Luxury..." Tyltyl said: "I am so sorry... I can't come for the moment. We are in a great hurry, we are looking for the Blue Bird. You don't happen to know, I suppose, where he is hiding?"

"Blue Bird? Wait a bit... Yes, I remember. He is a bird, that is not good to eat, I believe. At any rate, he has never figured on our table. That means that we have a poor opinion of him."

"What do you do for living?" Tyltyl asked.

"Why, we occupy ourselves incessantly in doing nothing. We never have a moment's rest. We have to drink, we have to eat, we have to sleep. It's most engrossing."

"Is it amusing?"

"Why, yes... It needs must be; it's all there is on this Earth." The Luxury of Being Rich replied.

"Do you think so?" asked Light.

The Luxury of Being Rich felt offended and pointed to Light. "Who is that ill-bred young person?"

Tyltyl suddenly saw some of his companion seated fraternally at the table with their hosts, eating, drinking and flinging themselves around wildly.

"Why, look, Light! They are sitting at the table!" cried Tyltyl.

"Turn the diamond, it is time!" Light instructed Tyltyl.

Tyltyl soon obeyed. Forthwith, all changed. The heavy ornaments in the foreground, the thick red hangings became unfastened and disappeared, revealing an immense and magnificent hall, a sort of cathedral of gladness and serenity, tall, innocent and almost transparent, whose endless fabric rests upon innumerable long and slender, limpid and blissful columns. The table of the orgy melted away without leaving a trace; the velvets, the brocades, the garlands of the Luxuries were torn asunder and fall, together with the grinning masks, at the feet of the astounded revelers. The Luxuries became visibly deflated, like burst bladders, exchanged glances, blinked their eyes in the unknown rays that hurt them. Seeing themselves at last as they really are, naked, hideous, flabby and lamentable, they began to uttered yells of shame and dismay.

Tyltyl watched the Luxuries flying around: "Goodness, how ugly they are! Where are they going?"

"I really believe that they have lost their heads. They are going to take refuge with the Miseries, where I very much fear that they will be kept for good." Said Light.

Tyltyl looked around wonder-struck. "Oh, what a beautiful hall! Where are we?"

"We have not moved. It is our eyes that see differently. We now behold the truth of things. And we shall perceive the soul of the Joys that endure the brightness of the diamond." Light explained to Tyltyl.

Tyltyl felt a little bit of lament: "How beautiful it is! Hullo! It looks as though people were coming to talk to us."

The halls began to fill with angel forms that seem to be emerging from a long slumber and glide harmoniously between the columns.

"Oh, what a lot of them there are! They are crowding from every side!" exclaimed Tyltyl.

Light said to Tyltyl: "There were many more of them once. The Luxuries have done them great harm."

"No matter, there are a good few of them left." Tyltyl consoled.

A troop of little Happiness, frisking and bursting with laughter, ran up and dance round the Children in a ring.

"How pretty, how very pretty they are! Where do they come from, who are they?" Tyltyl said with amazement.

"They are the Children's Happinesses."

Another troop of Happiness, a little taller than the last, rushed into the hall, singing at the top of their voice, "There they are! There they are!" and, danced a merry fling around the Children, at the end of which the one who appeared to be the chief of the little band went up to Tyltyl with hand outstretched.

"I am the chief of the Happinesses of your home; and all these are the other Happinesses that live there."

"There are Happinesses in my home?" asked Tyltyl embarrassedly. All the Happinesses burst out laughing.

The Happiness exclaimed loudly: "You heard him! Why, you little wretch, it is crammed with Happinesses in every nook and cranny! We laugh, we sing, we create enough joy to knock down the walls and lift the roof; but, do what we may, you see nothing and you hear nothing. Let me introduce myself first: the Happiness of Being Well, at your service. I am not the prettiest, but I am the most important. Will you know me again? This is the Happiness of Pure Air, who is almost transparent. Here is the Happiness of Loving one's Parents, who is clad in grey and always a little sad, because no one ever looks at him. Here are the Happiness of the Blue Sky, who, of course, is dressed in blue, and the Happiness of the Forest, who, also of course, is clad in green: you will see him every time you go to the

window. Here, again, is the good Happiness of Sunny Hours, who is diamond-colored, and this is the Happiness of Spring, who is bright emerald."

"And are you as fine as that every day?" asked Tyltyl.

The Happiness of Being Well: "Why, yes, it is Sunday every day, in every house, when people open their eyes. And then, when evening comes, here is the Happiness of the Sunsets, who is grander than all the kings in the world and who is followed by the Happiness of Seeing the Stars Rise, who is gilded like a god of old. Then, when the weather breaks, here are the Happiness of the Rain, who is covered with pearls, and the Happiness of the Winter Fire, who opens his beautiful purple mantle to frozen hands. And I have not mentioned the best among us, because he is nearly a brother of the great limpid Joys whom you will see presently: his name is the Happiness of Innocent Thoughts, and he is the brightest of as all... And then here are... But really there are too many of them! We should never have done; and I must first send word to the Great Joys, who are right at the back, near the gates of Heaven, and who have not yet heard of your arrival... I will send the Happiness of Running Barefoot in the Dew, who is the nimblest of us."

"Do you know where to find the Blue Bird?" Tyltyl inquired.

"He doesn't know where the Blue Bird is!" All the Happinesses of The Home burst out laughing.

Tyltyl got vexed: "No, I do not know. There's nothing to laugh at..."

"The purest Happiness that we have are here..." said chief of the Hapinesses to Tyltyl.

"Who is it?"

"Don't you recognize her yet? But take a better look at her, open your two eyes down to the very heart of your soul! She has seen you! She runs up to you, holding out her arms! It is your mother's Joy, it is the peerless Joy of Maternal Love!"

The other Joys, who had run up from every side, acclaimed the Joy of Maternal Love with their cheers and then fall back before her in silence.

"Tyltyl! And Mytyl! I never expected it! I was very lonely at home; and here are you two climbing to that Heaven where the souls of all mothers beam with joy! But first kisses, heaps and heaps of kisses! Into my arms, the two of you; there is nothing on earth that gives greater happiness!" cried the Joy of Maternal Love merrily.

"I did not know... You are like Mummy, but you are much prettier..." said Tyltyl unsurely.

"Why, of course, I have stopped growing old... And every day brings me fresh strength and youth and happiness. Each of your smiles makes me younger by a year."

Tyltyl were wonder-struck. He gazed at her and kissed her by turns. "And that beautiful dress of yours: what is it made of? Is it silk, silver or pearls?"

Maternal of Love said it with full of joy: "It is made of kisses and caresses and loving looks... Each kiss you give me adds a ray of moon-light or sunshine to it"

"How funny, I should never have thought that you were so rich! Where used you to hide it?"

"No, no, I always wear it, but people do not see it, because people see nothing when their eyes are closed. All mothers are rich when they love their children. There are no poor mothers, no ugly

ones, no old ones. Their love is always the most beautiful of the Joys...
And, when they seem most sad, it needs but a kiss which they receive
or give to turn all their tears into stars in the depths of their eyes."

Tyltyl looked at her with astonishment: "Why, yes, it's true, your
eyes are filled with stars. And they are really your eyes, only they are
much more beautiful. And this is your hand too, with the little ring on
it. It even has the burn which you gave it one evening when lighting
the lamp. But it is much whiter; and how delicate the skin is! There
seems to be light flowing through it... It's wonderful, Mummy: you
have the same voice also; but you speak much better than you do at
home..."

"You have come up here only to realize and to learn, once and
for all, how to see me when you see me down below. Do you
understand, Tyltyl dear? Heaven is wherever you and I kiss each other.
There are not two mothers; and you have no other. Every child has
only one; and it is always the same one and always the most beautiful;
but you have to know her and to know how to look..." explained the
Joy of Maternal Love patiently. "But how did you manage to come
up here and to find a road for which men have been seeking ever since
they began to dwell upon the Earth?"

Tyltyl pointed to Light. "It's Light. She brought me..."

Maternal Love embraced Light. "You have been very good to
my poor little ones..."

Light said: "I shall always be good to those who love one
another..."

They exchanged a long kiss; and, when they separated and raised
their heads, tears were seen to stand in their eyes.

Tyltyl seemed surprised and asked: "Why are you crying?" He

looked at the other Joys. "I say! You're crying too! But why have all of you tears in your eyes?"

"Hush, dear..." said Light to Tyltyl gently.

7

THE GRAVEYARD

When the Children were not going on an expedition, they played about in the Realms of Light. It was always summer there and never a moment was darkened by the night; but the hours were known by their different colors; there were pink, white, blue, lilac, green and yellow hours; and, according to their hues, the flowers, the fruits, the birds, the butterflies and the scents changed, causing Tyltyl and Mytyl a constant surprise. When they were tired of playing, they stretched themselves out on the backs of the lizards, which were as long and wide as little boats, and quickly, quickly raced round the garden paths, over the sand which was as white and as good to eat as sugar. When they were thirsty, Water shook her tresses into the cup of the enormous flowers; and the Children drank straight out of the lilies, tulips and morning-glories. If they were hungry, they picked radiant fruits which revealed the taste of Light to them and which had juice that shone like the rays of the sun.

There was also, in a clump of bushes, a white marble pond which possessed a magic power: its clear waters reflected not the faces, but the souls of those who looked into it.

"It's a ridiculous invention," said the Cat, who steadily refused to go near the pond. Tylo was not afraid to go and quench his thirst there: he need not fear to reveal his thoughts, for he was the only creature whose soul never altered. The dear Dog had no feelings but

those of love and kindness and devotion.

When Tyltyl bent over the magic mirror, he almost always saw the picture of a splendid Blue Bird, for the constant wish to find Blue Bird filled his mind entirely. Then he would run to Light and entreat her: "Tell me where he is! You know everything. Tell me where to find him!"

But she replied, in a tone of mystery: "I cannot tell you anything. You must find him for yourself." And, kissing him, she added, "Cheer up; you are getting nearer to him at each trial."

Now there came a day on which she said to him: "I have received a message from the Fairy Bérylune telling me that the Blue Bird is probably hidden in the graveyard. It appears that one of the Dead in the graveyard is keeping him in his tomb."

"What shall we do?" asked Tyltyl.

"It is very simple. At midnight you will turn the diamond and you shall see the Dead come out of the ground."

At these words, Milk, Water, Bread and Sugar began to yell and scream and chatter their teeth.

"Don't mind them," said Light to Tyltyl, in a whisper. "They are afraid of the Dead."

"I'm not afraid of them!" said Fire, frisking around. "Time was when I used to burn them; that was much more amusing than nowadays."

"Oh, I feel I am going to turn," wailed Milk.

"I'm not afraid," said the Dog, trembling in every limb, "but if you run away⋯ I shall run away too⋯ and with the greatest pleasure⋯"

The Cat sat pulling at her whiskers: "I know what's what," she said, in her usual mysterious way.

"Be quiet," said Light. "The Fairy gave strict orders. You are all to stay with me at the gate of the graveyard. The Children are to go in alone."

Tyltyl felt anything but pleased. He asked: "Aren't you coming with us?"

"No," said Light. "The time for that has not arrived. Light cannot yet enter among the Dead. Besides, there is nothing to fear. I shall not be far away."

She had not finished speaking, when everything around the Children changed. The wonderful temple; the dazzling flowers, the splendid gardens vanished to make way for a poor little country cemetery, which lay in the soft moonlight. Near the Children were a number of graves, grassy mounds, wooden crosses and tombstones. Tyltyl and Mytyl were seized with terror and hugged each other.

"I am frightened!" said Mytyl.

"I am never frightened," stammered Tyltyl, who was shaking with fear, but did not like to say so.

"Are the Dead wicked?" asked Mytyl.

"Why, no," said Tyltyl, "they're not alive!"

"Are we going to see them?"

Tyltyl shuddered at this question and made an unsuccessful effort to steady his voice as he answered: "Why, of course, Light said so!"

"Where are the Dead?" asked Mytyl.

Tyltyl cast a frightened look around him, for the Children had not dared to stir since they were alone.

"The Dead are here," he said, "under the grass or under those big stones."

"Are those the doors of their houses?" asked Mytyl, pointing to the tombstones.

"Yes."

"Do they go out when it's fine?"

"They can only go out at night."

"Is it nice in their homes?"

"They say it's very cramped."

"Have they any little children?"

"Why, yes, they have all those who die."

"And what do they live on?"

Tyltyl stopped to think. As the Dead live under ground, they can hardly eat anything that is above it; and so he answered very positively:

"They eat roots!"

Mytyl was quite satisfied and returned to the great question that was occupying her little mind:

"Shall we see them?" she asked.

"Of course," said Tyltyl, "we see everything when I turn the diamond."

A breath of wind made the leaves of the trees whisper and suddenly recalled the Children to their fears and their sense of loneliness. They hugged each other tight and began to talk again, so as

not to hear the horrible silence.

"When will you turn the diamond?" asked Mytyl.

"You heard Light say that I was to wait until midnight, because that disturbs them less; it is when they come out to take the air."

"Isn't it midnight yet"

Tyltyl turned round, saw the church clock and hardly had the strength to answer, for the hands were just upon the hour.

"Listen," he stammered, "listen⋯ It is just going to strike⋯ There! Do you hear?"

And the clock struck.

Then Mytyl, frightened out of her life, began to stamp her feet and utter piercing screams:

"I want to go away! I want to go away!"

Tyltyl, though stiff with fright, was able to say: "Not now. I am going to turn the diamond⋯"

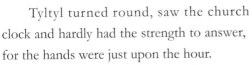

"No, no, no!" cried Mytyl. "I am so frightened, little brother! Don't do it! I want to go away!"

Tyltyl vainly tried to lift his hand but he could not reach the diamond with Mytyl clinging to him, hanging with all her weight on her brother's arm and screaming at the top of her voice: "I don't want to see the Dead! They will be awful! I can't possibly··· I am much too frightened!"

The eleventh stroke rang out.

"The hour is passing!" he exclaimed. "It is time!"

And releasing himself resolutely from Mytyl's arms, he turned the diamond···

A moment of terrible silence followed for the poor little children. Then they saw the crosses totter, the mounds open, the slabs rise up···

Mytyl hid her face against Tyltyl's chest.

"They're coming out!" she cried. "They're there! They're there!"

Tyltyl shut his eyes and only kept himself from fainting by leaning against a tree beside him. He remained like that for a minute that seemed to him like a century, not daring to move, not daring to breathe. Then he heard birds singing; a warm and scented breeze fanned his face; and, on his hands, on his neck, he felt the soft heat of the balmy summer sun. Now quite reassured, but unable to believe in so great a miracle, he opened his eyes and at once began to shout with happiness and admiration.

From all the open tombs came thousands of splendid flowers. They spread everywhere, on the paths, on the trees, on the grass; and they went up and up until it seemed that they would touch the sky. They were great full-blown roses, showing their hearts, wonderful golden hearts from which came the hot, bright rays which had wrapped Tyltyl in that summer warmth. Round the roses, birds sang and bees buzzed merrily.

"I can't believe it! It's not possible!" said Tyltyl. "What has become of the tombs and the stone crosses?"

Dazzled and bewildered, the two children walked hand in hand through the graveyard, of which not a trace remained, for there was nothing but a wonderful garden on every side. They had thought that ugly skeletons would rise from the earth and run after them, pulling horrid faces; they had imagined all sorts of awful things. And now, in the presence of the truth. They saw that there are no Dead and that Life goes on always, always, but under fresh forms. The fading rose sheds its pollen, which gives birth to other roses, and its scattered petals scent the air. The fruits come when the blossoms fall from the trees; and the dingy, hairy caterpillar turns into a brilliant butterfly.

Beautiful birds circled all round Tyltyl and Mytyl. There were no blue ones among them, but the two Children were so glad of their discovery that they asked for nothing more. Astonished and delighted, they kept on repeating: "There are no Dead! There are no Dead!"

As soon as Tyltyl and Mytyl were in bed, Light kissed them and faded away at once, so as not to disturb their sleep with the rays that always streamed from her beautiful self.

8

THE FOREST

It must have been about midnight, when Tyltyl, who was dreaming of the little Blue Children, felt a soft velvet paw pass to and fro over his face. He was surprised and sat up in bed in a bit of a fright; but he was soon reassured when he saw his friend Tylette's glowing eyes glittering in the dark.

"Hush!" said the Cat in his ear. "Hush! Don't wake anybody. If we can arrange to slip out without being seen, we shall catch the Blue Bird tonight."

"But," said the boy, kissing Tylette, "Light would be so glad to help us and besides I should be ashamed to disobey her."

"If you tell her," said the Cat, sharply, "all is lost, believe me. Do as I say; and the day is ours."

The treacherous Cat answered all his arguments, saying that the reason why he had not found the Blue Bird so far was just the fault of Light, who always brought brightness with her. Let the Children only go hunting by themselves, in the dark, and they would soon find all the Blue Birds that make men's happiness. Tyltyl was too weak to set his will against trickery. He allowed himself to be persuaded.

Tyltyl, Mytyl and Cat set out across the fields in the white light of the moon.

"This time," she declared, "we shall have the Blue Bird, I am sure of it! I asked all the Trees in the very oldest forest; they know him, because he hides among them. Then, in order to have everybody there, I sent the Rabbit to beat the assembly and call the principal Animals in the country." said Cat with excitement.

They reached the edge of the dark forest in an hour's time. Then, Tylette felt that her old time enemy seemed to be hurrying approach from the distance. She quivered with rage. Was he coming at the last moment, to save the Children's lives?

She leaned over to Tyltyl and whispered to him, in her most honeyed voice:

"I am sorry to say it is our worthy friend the Dog. It is a thousand pities, because his presence will make us fail in our object. He is on the worst of terms with everybody, even the Trees. Do tell him to go back!"

"Go away, we don't want you here. You're a nuisance!" said Tyltyl, shaking his fist at the Dog.

Poor Tylo was much hurt by these hard words. He was an obedient animal and, at any other time, he would have gone. But his affection told him what a serious business it was and he stood stock still.

"Do you allow this disobedience?" said the Cat to Tyltyl, in a whisper. "Hit him with your stick."

"No, no; I want him to stay," Mytyl pleaded. "I'm frightened when Tylo's not with us."

Time was short and they had to come to a decision.

"I'll find some other way to get rid of the idiot!" thought the Cat. And, turning to the Dog, she said, in her most gracious manner, "We shall be so pleased if you will join us!"

As they entered the great forest, the Children stuck close together, with the Cat and the Dog on either side of them. They were awed by the silence and the darkness and they felt much relieved when the Cat exclaimed: "Here we are! Turn the diamond!"

Then the light spread around them and showed them a wonderful sight. They were standing in the middle of a large round space in the heart of the forest, where all the old, old Trees seemed to reach up to the sky. Everything was peaceful and still; but suddenly a strange shiver ran through the foliage; the branches moved and stretched like human arms; the roots raised the earth that covered them, came together, took the shapes of legs and feet and stood on the ground; a tremendous crash rang through the air; the trunks of the Trees burst open and each of them let out its soul, which made its appearance like a funny human figure.

And Tylette introduced the soul of each Tree to him. There was the Elm, who was a sort of short-winded, paunchy, crabby gnome; the Beech, an elegant, sprightly person; the Birch, who looked like the ghosts in the Palace of Night, with his white flowing garments and his restless gestures. The tallest figure was the Fir-tree. Tyltyl found it very difficult to see his face perched right at the top of his long, thin body. But he looked gentle and sad, whereas the Cypress, who stood near him, dressed all in black, frightened Tyltyl terribly.

The Trees, delighted at being able to talk, were all chattering together; and Tyltyl was simply going to ask them where the Blue Bird was hidden, when, all of a sudden, silence reigned. The Trees bowed respectfully and stood aside to make way for an immensely old Tree, dressed in a long gown embroidered with moss and lichen. He leaned with one hand on a stick and with the other on a young Oak Sapling who acted as his guide, for the Old Oak was blind. His long white beard streamed in the wind.

"It's the King!" said Tyltyl to himself, when he saw his mistletoe crown. "I will ask him the secret of the forest."

And he was just going up to him, when he stopped, seized with surprise and joy: there sat the Blue Bird before him, perched on the old Oak's shoulder.

"He has the Blue Bird!" cried the boy, gleefully. "Quick! Quick! Give him to me!"

"Silence! Hold your tongue!" said the greatly shocked Trees.

"Take off your hat, Tyltyl," said the Cat. "It's the Oak!"

The poor Child at once obeyed with a smile; he did not understand the danger that threatened him and he did not hesitate to answer, "Yes, Sir," when the Oak asked him if he was the

woodcutter's son.

Then the Oak, trembling with rage, began to lay a terrible charge against Daddy: "In my family alone," he said, "your father has put to death six hundreds of my sons, four hundred and seventy-five uncles and aunts, twelve hundred cousins of both sexes, three hundred and eighty daughters-in-law and twelve thousand great-grandsons!"

"It's for the Fairy Bérylune's little girl, who is very ill," Tyltyl continued.

"Enough!" said the Oak, silencing him. "I do not hear the Animals. Where are they? All this concerns them as much as us. We, the Trees, must not assume the responsibility alone for the grave measures that have become necessary."

"Here they come!" said the Fir-tree, looking over the top of the other Trees. "They are following the Rabbit. I can see the souls of the Horse, the Bull, the Ox, the Cow, the Wolf, the Sheep, the Pig, the Goat, and the Bear."

All the Animals now arrived. They walked on their hind-legs and were dressed like human beings. They solemnly took up their positions in a circle among the Trees, all except the frivolous Goat, who began to skip down the avenues, and the Pig, who hoped to find some glorious truffles among the roots that had newly left the ground.

"Are all here present?" asked the Oak.

"Aren't they funny? They are just like the rich children's fine toys in the windows at Christmas time." Tyltyl whispered to Mytyl.

"The child you see before you," said the Oak, "thanks to a talisman stolen from the powers of Earth, is able to take possession of our Blue Bird and thus to snatch from us the secret which we have

kept since the origin of life⋯ Now we know enough of Man to entertain no doubt as to the fate which he reserves for us, once he is in possession of this secret. Any hesitation would be both foolish and criminal. It is a serious moment; the child must be done away with before it is too late⋯"

"What is be saying?" asked Tyltyl, who could not make out what the old Tree was driving at.

The Dog was prowling round the Oak and now showed his fangs:

"Do you see my teeth, you old cripple?" he growled.

"He is insulting the Oak!" said the Beech indignantly.

"Drive him out!" shouted the Oak, angrily. "He's a traitor!"

"What did I tell you?" whispered the Cat to Tyltyl. "I will arrange things. But send him away."

"Will you be off!" said Tyltyl to the Dog.

"Do let me worry the gouty old beggar's moss slippers!" begged Tylo.

Tyltyl tried in vain to prevent him. The rage of Tylo, who understood the danger, knew no bounds. Cat called in the Ivy, and the Dog pranced about like a madman, abusing everybody. He railed at the Ivy: "Come on, if you dare, you old ball of twine, you!"

The onlookers growled. The Oak was pale with fury at seeing his authority denied. But Tyltyl threatened Tylo harshly and the Dog lay down at his master's feet out of obedience. From that moment, the Children were lost. The Ivy gagged and bound the poor Dog, who was then taken behind the Chestnut-tree and tied to his biggest root.

"Now," cried the Oak, in a voice of thunder, "we can take counsel, quietly. This is the first time that it is given us to judge Man! I do not think that, after the monstrous injustice which we have suffered, there can remain the least doubt as to the sentence that awaits him."

One cry rang from every throat: "Death! Death! Death!"

The poor Children did not at first understand their doom.

"What is the matter with them?" asked the boy. "Are they displeased?"

"Don't be alarmed," said the Cat. "They are a little annoyed because Spring is late." And she went on talking into Tyltyl's ear, to divert his attention from what was happening.

While the trusting lad was listening to her fibs, the others were discussing which form of execution would be the most practical and the least dangerous. The Bull suggested a good butt with the horns; the Beech offered his highest branch to hang the little Children on; and the Ivy was already preparing a slipknot! The Fir-tree was willing to give the four planks for the coffin and the Cypress the perpetual grant of a tomb.

"By far the simplest way," whispered the Willow, "would be to drown them in one of my rivers."

And the Pig grunted between his teeth: "In my opinion, the great thing would be to eat the little girl··· She ought to be very tender."

"Silence!" roared the Oak. "What we have to decide is which of us shall have the honor of striking the first blow!"

"That honor falls to you, our King!" said the Fir-tree.

"Alas, I am too old!" replied the Oak. "I am blind and infirm! To you, be the glory of striking the decisive blow that shall set us free."

But the Fir-tree declined the honor. He suggested the Beech, as owning the best club.

"It is out of the question," said the Beech. "You know I am worm-eaten! Ask the Elm and the Cypress."

Thereupon the Elm began to moan and groan: a mole had twisted his great toe the night before and he could hardly stand upright; and the Cypress excused himself and so did the Poplar, who declared that he was ill and shivering with fever.

Then the Oak's indignation flared up: "You are afraid of Man!" he exclaimed. "Even those unprotected and unarmed little Children inspire you with terror! Well, I shall do it by myself. Where are them?"

And groping his way with his stick, he moved towards Tyltyl, growling as he went.

Tyltyl had been very much afraid during the last few minutes. The Cat had left him suddenly, saying that she wanted to smooth down the excitement, and had not come back. Mytyl nestled trembling against him; and he felt very lonely. When he saw the Oak marching on him with a threatening air, he drew his pocket-knife and defied him like a man.

"Is it I he's after, that old one, with his big stick?" Tyltyl cried.

But, at the sight of the knife, Man's irresistible weapon, all the Trees shook with fright and rushed at the Oak to hold him back. There was a struggle; and the old King, conquered by the weight of years, threw away his stick.

"Shame on us." Oak shouted. "Shame on us! Let the Animals deliver us!"

Mytyl uttered piercing screams.

"Don't be afraid," said Tyltyl, doing his best to protect her. "I have my knife."

"The little chap means to die game!" said the Cock.

"That's the one I shall eat first," said the Pig, eyeing Mytyl greedily.

"What have I done to all of you?" asked Tyltyl.

"Nothing at all, my little man," said the Sheep. "Eaten my little brother, my two sisters, my three uncles, my aunt, my grandpapa and my grandmarnma··· Wait, wait, when you're down, you shall see that I have teeth also."

While they were talking, the Wolf and the Bear treacherously attacked Tyltyl from behind and pushed him over. It was an awful moment. All the Animals, seeing him on the ground, tried to get at him. The boy raised himself to one knee and brandished his knife. Mytyl uttered yells of distress. And, to crown all, it suddenly became dark.

Tyltyl called wildly for assistance: "Help! Help! Tylo! Tylo! To the rescue! Where is Tylette? Come! Come!"

The Cat's voice was heard in the distance, where she was craftily keeping out of sight: "I can't come!" she whined. "I'm wounded!"

All this time, plucky little Tyltyl was defending himself as best he could, but he was alone against all of them, felt that he was going to be killed and, in a faltering voice, cried once more:

"Help! Tylo! Tylo! I can't hold out! There are too many of them!"

Then the Dog came leaping along, dragging his broken bonds and elbowing his way through the Trees and Animals and flung himself before his master, whom he defended furiously.

"Here, my little god! Don't be afraid! Have at them! I know how

to use my teeth!"

Tyltyl vainly tried to defend himself.

"I'm done for, Tylo! It was a blow from the Elm! My hand's bleeding!" And he dropped to the ground. "No, I can hold out no longer!"

"They are coming!" said the Dog. "I hear somebody! We are saved! It is Light! Saved! Saved! See, they're afraid, they're retreating! Saved, my little king!"

And, sure enough, Light was coming towards them; and with her the dawn rose over the forest, which became light as day.

"What is it? What has happened?" she asked, quite alarmed at the sight of the little ones and their dear Tylo covered with wounds and bruises. "Why, my poor boy, didn't you know? Turn the diamond quickly!"

Tyltyl hastened to obey; and immediately the souls of all the Trees rushed back into their trunks, which closed upon them. The souls of the Animals also disappeared; and there was nothing to be seen but a cow and a sheep browsing peacefully in the distance. The forest became harmless once more. And Tyltyl looked around him in amazement.

"No matter," he said, "but for the Dog⋯ and if I hadn't had my knife!"

Light thought that he had been punished enough and did not scold him. Besides, she was very much upset by the horrible danger which he had run.

Tyltyl, Mytyl and the Dog, glad to meet again safe and sound, exchanged Wild kisses. They laughingly counted their wounds, which were not very serious.

Tylette was the only one to make a fuss: "The Dog's broken my paw!" she mewed.

Tylo felt as if he could have made a mouthful of her: "Never mind!" he said. "It'll keep!"

"Leave her alone, will you, you ugly beast?" said Mytyl.

Tyltyl, repenting of his disobedience, dared not even mention the Blue Bird of which he had caught a glimpse; and Light said to the Children, gently: "Let this teach you, dears, that Man is all alone against all in this world. Never forget that."

9

THE LEAVE-TAKING

Weeks and months had passed since the children's departure on their journey; and the hour of separation was at hand.

On the day, they were all out in the gardens of the temple. Light stood watching them from a marble terrace, with Tyltyl and Mytyl sleeping by her side. Bread had eaten so much that he was now not able to walk: Milk, devoted as ever, dragged him along in a Bath chair. Fire's nasty temper had made him quarrel with everybody and he had become very lonely and unhappy in consequence. Water, who had no will of her own, had ended by yielding to Sugar's sweet entreaties: they were now married; and Sugar presented a most piteous sight. The poor fellow was reduced to a shadow of his former self, shrank visibly day by day and was sillier than ever, while Water, in marrying, had lost her principal charm, her simplicity. The Cat had remained the liar that she always was; and our dear friend Tylo had never been able to overcome his hatred for her.

"Poor things!" thought Light, with a sigh. "They have not gained much by receiving the benefit of life! They were either quarrelling with one another or over-eating themselves. They will recognize the happiness for the first time presently, when they are about to lose it."

At that moment, a pretty dove, with silver wings, alighted on her knees. It wore an emerald collar round its neck, with a note fastened

to the clasp. The dove was the Fairy Bérylune's messenger. Light opened the letter and read these few words: "Remember that the year is over."

Then Light stood up, waved her wand and everything disappeared from sight.

A few seconds later, the whole company were gathered together outside a high wall with a small door in it. The first rays of the dawn were gilding the tree-tops. Tyltyl and Mytyl, whom Light was fondly supporting with her arms, woke up, rubbed their eyes and looked around them in astonishment.

"What?" said Light to Tyltyl. "Don't you know that wall and that little door?"

The sleepy boy shook his head: he remembered nothing.

Then Light assisted his memory: "The wall," she said, "surrounds a house which we left one evening just a year ago today."

"Just a year ago? Why, then····" And, clapping his hands with glee, Tyltyl ran to the door. "We must be near Mummy! I want to kiss her at once, at once, at once!"

But Light stopped him. It was too early, she said: Mummy and Daddy were still asleep and he must not wake them with a start.

"Besides," she added, "the door will not open till the hour strikes."

"What hour?" asked the boy.

"The hour of separation," Light answered, sadly.

"What!" said Tyltyl, in great distress. "Are you leaving us?"

"I must," said Light. "The year is past. The Fairy will come back and ask you for the Blue Bird."

"But I haven't got the Blue Bird!" cried Tyltyl. "The one of the Land of Memory turned quite black, the one of the Future flew away, the Night's are dead, those in the Graveyard were not blue and I could not catch the one in the Forest! Will the Fairy be angry? What will she say?"

"Never mind, dear," said Light. "You did your best. And, though you did not find the Blue Bird, you deserved to do so, for the good will, pluck and courage which you showed."

Light's face beamed with happiness as she spoke these words. She turned to the Animals and Things, who stood weeping in a corner, and told them to come and kiss the Children.

"The hour is passing... Be quick and say good-bye to the Children." said Light.

Fire rushed forward, took hold of the Children, one after the other, and kissed them so violently that they screamed with pain: "Oh! Oh! He's burning me!"

"Oh! Oh! He's scorched my nose!"

"Let me kiss the place and make it well," said Water, going up to the children gently.

This gave Fire his chance: "Take care," he said, "you'll get wet."

"I am loving and gentle," said Water. "I am kind to human beings."

"What about those you drown?" asked Fire.

But Water pretended not to hear: "Love the wells, listen to the brooks," she said. "I shall always be there. When you sit down in the evening, beside the springs, try to understand what they are trying to say."

Then she had to break off, for a regular waterfall of tears came gushing from her eyes, flooding all around her. However, she resumed:

"Think of me when you see the water bottle. You will find me also in the ewer, the watering can, the cistern and the tap."

Then Sugar came up, with a limping walk, for he could hardly stand on his feet. He uttered a few words of sorrow, in an affected voice and then stopped, for tears, he said, were not in harmony with his temperament.

"Humbug!" cried Bread.

"Sugar plum! Lollipop! Caramel!" yelped Fire.

And all began to laugh, except the two children, who were very sad:

"Where are Tylette and Tylo gone to?" asked our hero.

At that moment, the Cat came running up, in a terrible state: her hair was on end and disheveled, her clothes were torn and she was holding a handkerchief to her cheek, as though she had the tooth-ache. She uttered terrible groans and was closely pursued by the Dog, who overwhelmed her with bites, blows and kicks.

"You've had some," Dog kept saying, "you've had some and you're going to have some more!"

But, suddenly his tongue turned quite white when Light told him to kiss the Children for the last time.

"For the last time?" stammered poor Tylo. "Are we to part from these poor Children?"

His grief was such that he was incapable of understanding anything.

"Yes," said Light. "The hour which you know of is at hand. We are going to return to silence."

THE LEAVE-TAKING

Thereupon the Dog began to utter real howls of despair and fling himself upon the Children, whom he loaded with mad and violent caresses.

"No! No!" he cried. "I refuse! I refuse! I shall always talk! I shall learn to read and write and play dominoes! And I shall always be very clean. And I shall never steal anything in the kitchen again."

He went on his knees before the two Children, sobbing and entreating, and, when Tyltyl, with his eyes full of tears, remained silent. Then Mytyl said, innocently: "You, Tylette, are the only one that hasn't kissed us yet."

The Cat put on a mincing tone:

"Children," said she, "I love you both as much as you deserve."

There was a pause.

"And now," said Light, "let me, in my turn, give you a last kiss."

As she spoke, she spread her veil round them as if she would have wrapped them for the last time in her luminous might. Then she gave them each a long and loving kiss. Tyltyl and Mytyl hung on to her beseechingly:

"No, no, no, Light!" they cried. "Stay here with us! Daddy won't mind. We will tell Mummy how kind you have been."

But Light quieted them with a motherly gesture and said words to them which they never forgot.

"Listen, Tyltyl. Do not forget, child, that everything that you see in this world has neither beginning nor end. If you keep this thought in your heart and let it grow up with you, you will always, in all circumstances, know what to say, what to do and what to hope for."

195

 Chapter 9

And, when our two friends began to sob, she added, lovingly: "Do not cry, my dear little ones. I have not a voice like Water; I have only my brightness, which Man does not understand. But I watch over him to the end of his days. Never forget that I am speaking to you in every spreading moonbeam, in every twinkling star, in every dawn that rises, in every lamp that is lit, in every good and bright thought of your soul."

At that moment, the grandfather's clock in the cottage struck eight o' clock. Light, in a voice that grew suddenly fainter, whispered: "Good bye! Good bye! The hour is striking! Good bye!"

Her figure vanished and, through their tears, the Children saw nothing but a thin ray of light dying away at their feet. the others were all disappeared.

10

THE AWAKENING

The grandfather's clock in the woodcutter's cottage had struck eight; and his two little Children, Tyltyl and Mytyl, were still asleep in their little beds. Mummy stood looking at them, with her arms akimbo and her apron tucked up, laughing and scolding in the same breath:

"I can't let them go on sleeping till midday," she said. "Come, get up, you little lazybones!"

After receiving a gentle thump in the ribs, Tyltyl opened his eyes and murmured: "What? Light? Where, are you? No, no, don't go away."

"Light!" cried Mummy, laughing. "Why, of course, it's light. Has been for ever so long!"

"Mummy! Mummy!" said Tyltyl, rubbing his eyes. "It's you!" He was beside himself with delight! It was ages and ages since he had seen his Mummy and he never tired of kissing her.

Mummy began to be uneasy. Here her boy was suddenly talking of a long journey in the company of the Fairy and Water and Milk and Sugar and Fire and Bread and Light! He made believe that he had been away a year!

"But you haven't left the room!" cried Mummy, who was now nearly beside herself with fright. "I put you to bed last night and here you are this morning! It's Christmas Day: don't you hear the bells in the village?"

"I went away a year ago, on Christmas Eve!" said Tyltyl, obstinately, "You're not angry with me? Did you feel very sad? And what did Daddy say?"

The little boy rattled on: "Ask Mytyl, if you don't believe me. Oh, we have had such adventures! We saw Grandpa and Granny... yes, in the Land of Memory, it was on our way. They are dead, but they are quite well, aren't they, Mytyl?"

And Mytyl, who was now beginning to wake up, joined her brother in describing their visit to the grandparents and the fun which they had had with their little brothers and sisters.

Mummy ran to the door of the cottage and called with all her might to her husband, who was working on the edge of the forest:

"Oh, dear, oh, dear!" she cried. "I shall lose them as I lost the others! Do come! Come quick."

Daddy soon entered the cottage, with his axe in his hand. The two Children told the story of their adventures over again and asked him what he had done during the year.

"You see, you see!" said Mummy, crying. "They have lost their heads, something will happen to them; run and fetch the doctor."

But the woodcutter was not the man to put himself out for such a trifle. He kissed the little ones, calmly lit his pipe and declared that they looked very well and that there was no hurry.

At that moment, there came a knock at the door and the neighbor walked in. She was a little old woman leaning on a stick and very much like the Fairy Bérylune. The Children at once flung their arms around her neck and capered round her, shouting merrily: "It's the Fairy Bérylune!"

The neighbor said to Mummy: "I have come to ask for a bit of fire for my Christmas stew. It's very chilly this morning. Good morning, children."

Meanwhile, Tyltyl had become a little thoughtful. He made up his mind like a man and went up to her boldly: "Fairy Bérylune, I could not find the Blue Bird."

"What is he saying?" asked the neighbor, quite taken aback. "Béry... what?"

"Bérylune," answered Tyltyl, calmly.

"Berlingot," said the neighbor. "You mean Berlingot."

Tyltyl was a little put out by her positive way of talking; and he answered: "Bérylune or Berlingot, as you please, ma' am, but I know what I'm saying."

Daddy was beginning to have enough of it. "We must put a stop to this," he said. "I will give them a smack or two."

"Don't," said the neighbor: "it's not worthwhile. It's only a little fit of dreaming; they must have been sleeping in the moonbeams. My little girl, who is very ill, is often like that." said the neighbor, shaking her head. "The doctor says it's her nerves. I know what would cure her, for all that. She was asking me for it only this morning, for her Christmas present."

She hesitated a little, looked at Tyltyl with a sigh and added, in a disheartened tone: "What can I do? It's a fancy she has..."

The others knew what the neighbor's words meant. Her little girl had long been saying that she would get well if Tyltyl would only give her his dove; but he was so fond of it that he refused to part with it.

"Well," said Mummy to her son, "won't you give your bird to that poor little thing? She has been dying to have it for so long!"

"My bird!" cried Tyltyl, slapping his forehead as though they had spoken of something quite out of the way. "My bird!" He took a chair, put it under the cage and climbed on to it gaily, saying: "Of course, I'll give him to her, of course, I will!"

Then he stopped, in amazement: "Why, he's blue!" he said. "It's my dove, just the same, but he has turned blue while I was away!"

And Tyltyl jumped down from the chair and began to skip for joy, crying: "It's the Blue Bird we were looking for! We have been miles and miles and miles and he was here all the time! He was here, at home! Oh, but how wonderful! Mytyl, do you see the bird? What would Light say? There, Madame Berlingot, take him quickly to your little girl."

Neighbor Berlingot beamed all over her face, clasped her hands together and mumbled her thanks. She hugged the boy in her arms and wept with joy and gratitude: "Do you give it me?" she kept saying. "Do you give it me like that, straight away and for nothing? Goodness, how happy she will be! I fly, I fly! I will come back to tell you what she says."

"Yes, yes, go quickly," 'said Tyltyl, "for some of them change their color!"

Neighbor Berlingot ran out and Tyltyl shut the door after her. Then he thought everything more beautiful, for, to his richer and purer understanding, everything must needs seem infinitely fairer than before.

Meanwhile, Tyltyl continued his joyful inspection of the cottage. He leaned over the bread-pan to speak a kind word to the Loaves; he rushed at Tylo, who was sleeping in his basket, and congratulated him

on the good fight which he had made in the forest.

Mytyl stooped down to stroke Tylette, who was snoozing by the stove, and said: "Well, Tylette? You know me, I see, but you have stopped talking."

Then Tyltyl put his hand up to his forehead. "Hullo!" he cried. "The diamond's gone! Who's taken my little green hat? Never mind, I don't want it anymore! Ah, there's Fire! Good morning, sir! He'll be crackling to make Water angry!" He ran to the tap, turned it on and bent down over the water. "Good morning, Water, good morning! What does she say? She still talks, but I don't understand her as well as I did. Oh, how happy I am, how happy I am!"

"So am I, so am I!" cried Mytyl.

And they took each other's hands and began to scamper round the kitchen.

Mummy felt a little relieved at seeing them so full of life and spirits. Besides, Daddy was so calm and placid. He sat eating his porridge and laughing.

"You see, they are playing at being happy!" he said.

A wonderful dream had taught his little children not to play at being happy, but to be happy, which is the greatest and most difficult of lessons.

"You can see her over there, through the trees of the forest..." said Tyltyl to Mytyl, standing on tip-toe by the window.

He stopped and listened. Everybody lent an ear. They heard laughter and merry voices; and the sounds came nearer.

"It's her voice!" cried Tyltyl. "Let me open the door!"

As a matter of fact, it was the little girl, with her mother, Neighbor Berlingot.

"Look at her," said Goody Berlingot, quite overcome with joy. "She can run, she can dance, and she can fly! It's a miracle! When she saw the bird, she jumped, just like that."

And Goody Berlingot hopped from one leg to the other at the risk of falling and breaking her long, hooked nose.

The Children clapped their hands and everybody laughed.

The little girl was there, in her long white night-dress, standing in the middle of the kitchen, a little surprised to find herself on her feet so many months' illness. She smiled and pressed Tyltyl's dove to her heart.

Tyltyl looked first at the child and then at Mytyl: "Don't you think she's very like Light?" he asked.

"She is much smaller," said Mytyl.

"Yes, indeed!" said Tylryl. "But she will grow!"

And the three Children tried to put a little food down the Bird's beak, while the parents began to feel easier in their minds and looked at them and smiled.

Tyltyl was radiant. The Dove had hardly changed color at all and that it was joy and happiness that decked him with a magnificent bright blue plumage in Tyltyl's eyes. No matter! Tyltyl, without knowing it, had discovered Light's great secret, which is that we draw nearer to happiness by trying to give it to others.

But now everybody became excited, the Children screamed, the parents threw up their arms and rushed to the open door: the Bird had suddenly escaped! He was flying away as fast as he could.

"My bird! My bird!" sobbed the little girl.

But Tyltyl was the first to run to the staircase and he returned in triumph: "It's all right!" he said. "Don't cry! He is still in the house and we shall find him again."

And he gave a kiss to the little girl, who was already smiling through her tears: "You'll be sure to catch him again, won't you?" she asked.

"Trust me," replied our friend, confidently. "I now know where he is."

You also, my dear little readers, now know where the Blue Bird is.

國家圖書館出版品預行編目 (CIP) 資料

青鳥（中英雙語典藏版）/ 莫里斯·梅特林克（Maurice
Maeterlinck）著；喬治特·萊勃倫克（Georgette
Leblanc）改編；詹艷玲繪；肖俊風譯. -- 二版. -- 臺
中市：晨星出版有限公司, 2024.07
　面；　公分. --（愛藏本：120）
中英雙語典藏版
譯自：L'Oiseau Bleu

ISBN 978-626-320-868-1（精裝）

881.759　　　　　　　　　　　113007573

愛藏本：120

青鳥（中英雙語典藏版）
L'Oiseau Bleu

作　　者｜莫里斯·梅特林克（Maurice Maeterlinck）
改　　編｜喬治特·萊勃倫克（Georgette Leblanc）
繪　　者｜詹艷玲
譯　　者｜肖俊風

執行編輯｜李迎華
封面設計｜李美瑤
美術編輯｜黃偵瑜
文字校潤｜李迎華

填寫線上回函，立即
獲得 50 元購書金。

創 辦 人｜陳銘民
發 行 所｜晨星出版有限公司
　　　　　台中市 407 工業區 30 路 1 號 1 樓
　　　　　TEL:(04)23595820　FAX:(04)23550581
　　　　　http://star.morningstar.com.tw
　　　　　行政院新聞局局版台業字第 2500 號
法律顧問｜陳思成律師
服務專線｜TEL:（02）23672044 /（04）23595819#212
傳真專線｜FAX:（02）23635741 /（04）23595493
讀者信箱｜service@morningstar.com.tw
網路書店｜http://www.morningstar.com.tw
郵政劃撥｜15060393（知己圖書股份有限公司）

初版日期｜2018 年 01 月 01 日
二版日期｜2024 年 07 月 15 日
　ISBN｜978-626-320-868-1
　定價｜新台幣 250 元

印　　刷｜上好印刷股份有限公司